"I want you to marry me," Mateo said again. "But let me explain."

"O...kay."

"I'm not who you think I am."

Now this was really beginning to seem melodramatic. Rachel had a sudden urge to laugh. "Okay," she said. "Who are you?"

"My full name and title? Prince Mateo Aegeus Karavitis, heir to the throne of the island kingdom of Kallyria."

Rachel stared at him dumbly. He had to be joking. Mateo had liked to play a practical joke or two back in the lab. Was that what he was doing here? Was he making fun of her? Her cheeks stung with mortification at the thought, and her heart felt as if it were shriveling inside her. *Please, no...*

"I'm sorry," she said stiffly. "I don't get it."

Mateo frowned, the dark slashes of his brows drawing together. Why did he have to be so handsome? Rachel wondered irritably. It didn't make this any easier or less painful. "Get it?"

"The punch line," she said flatly.

"There's no punch line, Rachel. I mean it. I accept this comes as a surprise, and it's not the most romantic proposal of marriage, but please let me explain..."

After spending three years as a die-hard New Yorker, **Kate Hewitt** now lives in a small village in the English Lake District with her husband, their five children and a golden retriever. In addition to writing intensely emotional stories, she loves reading, baking and playing chess with her son—she has yet to win against him, but she continues to try. Learn more about Kate at kate-hewitt.com.

Books by Kate Hewitt

Harlequin Presents

The Innocent's One-Night Surrender
Claiming My Bride of Convenience

Conveniently Wed!

Desert Prince's Stolen Bride

One Night With Consequences

Engaged for Her Enemy's Heir
Princess's Nine-Month Secret
Greek's Baby of Redemption

Secret Heirs of Billionaires

The Secret Kept from the Italian
The Italian's Unexpected Baby

Seduced by a Sheikh

The Secret Heir of Alazar
The Forced Bride of Alazar

Visit the Author Profile page
at Harlequin.com for more titles.

If you fell in love with
Vows to Save His Crown,
you're sure to adore
these other stories
by Kate Hewitt!

The Secret Kept from the Italian
Greek's Baby of Redemption
Claiming My Bride of Convenience
The Italian's Unexpected Baby

Available now!

Kate Hewitt

VOWS TO SAVE HIS CROWN

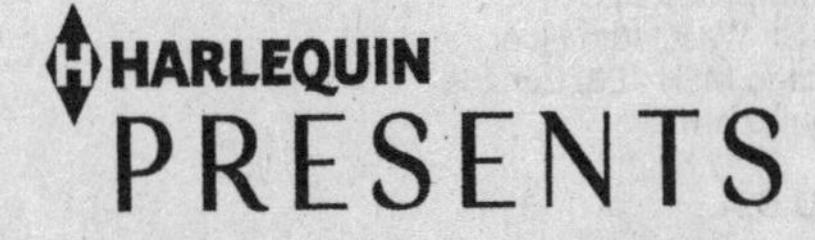

Recycling programs for this product may not exist in your area.

ISBN-13: 978-1-335-89382-6

Vows to Save His Crown

This is a work of fiction. Names, characters, places and incidents are either the product of the author's imagination or are used fictitiously. Any resemblance to actual persons, living or dead, businesses, companies, events or locales is entirely coincidental.

This edition published by arrangement with Harlequin Books S.A.

For questions and comments about the quality of this book, please contact us at CustomerService@Harlequin.com.

Harlequin Enterprises ULC
22 Adelaide St. West, 40th Floor
Toronto, Ontario M5H 4E3, Canada
www.Harlequin.com

Printed in U.S.A.

VOWS TO SAVE HIS CROWN

To Cliff, my partner and my prince! Love, K.

CHAPTER ONE

'I'M SORRY, MATEO.'

On the computer screen, Mateo Karavitis' mother's elegant face was drawn into weary lines of sadness and resignation—sadness for the position she'd put him in, and resignation that it had come to this. A queen who'd had three healthy, robust sons, an heir and *two* spares, and yet here he was, the unneeded third to the throne, now about to be thrust into the unwanted limelight.

'I know you don't want this,' his mother, Queen Agathe, continued quietly.

Mateo did not reply. He knew who didn't want this: his *mother*. How could she? As the third son, and a late surprise at that, he hadn't been prepared for the throne. He'd never been meant to be King, to rule Kallyria with a gentle manner and an iron fist the way his father had for thirty years, as a revered ruler, kind but strong, beloved by his people, feared by his enemies.

It has been his oldest brother Kosmos who had

been taken into training from infancy, told from the cradle who he was and what he would become. Kosmos who had gone to military school, who had met dignitaries and diplomats when he was barely out of nappies, who had been crowned Prince and heir to the throne when he was just fourteen, arrogantly assuming the title that would be his. And it was Kosmos who had died in a sailing accident ten years ago, when he was only thirty.

His oldest brother's sudden death had shocked his family to the core, and rocked its seemingly stable foundations. His father, King Barak, had diminished visibly in what felt like minutes, his powerful frame suddenly seeming smaller, the thick mane of grey hair turning thin and white. Three months after Kosmos' death, Barak had suffered a mini stroke that had affected his speech and movement but kept him on the throne. Four destabilising years after that, he'd died, aged only sixty-eight, and Mateo's older brother Leo, the true spare, had been crowned King.

How had they got here?

'Have you spoken to Leo?' he asked his mother, his tone brusque. 'Has he given an explanation for his unprecedented actions?'

'He…he just can't do it.' Agathe's voice, normally mellifluous and assured, wavered and broke. 'He's not up to it, Mateo. Not up to anything any more.'

'He is *King*.'

'Not any more,' she reminded him gently. 'Not since he abdicated last night.'

Mateo spun his chair around, hiding his face from his mother, a welter of emotions tangled inside him, too knotted up to discern one from the other. He'd never expected this. Even after Kosmos had died, after his father had died, he'd never expected this. Leo had seemed more than ready to assume their father's mantle. Leo, who had always been in Kosmos' shadow, finally ready to shine. He'd been more than ready for it, eager even. Mateo recalled the gleam in his brother's eye at their father's funeral, and it had sickened him. He'd walked away from Kallyria, intent on pursuing his own life here in England, away from the royal family and all its pressures.

And now he had to come back, because Leo was the one who was walking away. His brother had been King for more than half a decade, Mateo acknowledged with an iron-edged frustration. How could he just walk away from it all? Where was his sense of duty, of honour?

'I don't understand,' he ground out through gritted teeth. 'This is coming from nowhere.'

'Not nowhere.' Agathe's voice was soft and

sad. 'Your brother…he has always struggled to assume his royal duties.'

'Struggled?' His brother hadn't struggled when he'd practically snatched the crown from their father's head. 'He seemed more than ready to become King six years ago.'

Agathe's mouth tightened. 'The reality was far more challenging than the dream.'

'Isn't it always?' If his brother had acted as if being King was a licence to indulge whatever pleasures and whims he had…but Mateo didn't know if he had or not, because he'd chosen to distance himself from Kallyria and all it meant, and that had been fine by everyone, because until now he'd never been needed. 'How has he struggled, exactly?' He turned back to face Agathe, wanting to see the expression on her face.

She shrugged her slim shoulders and spread her manicured hands, her face drawn in lines of weary sorrow. 'You know Leo has always been a bit more highly strung than Kosmos. A bit more sensitive. He feels things deeply. He hides behind his pleasures.' Mateo made a dismissive sound. Leo was thirty-eight years old and had been reigning as King for nearly six. Surely it was more than time to put such boyish indulgences behind him, and act like a man. Like a king. 'With the insurgency in the north of the island,' Agathe continued, 'and the economic talks coming up that are so important…' She sighed sadly. 'He fell apart, Mateo. He simply fell apart. It was a long time coming, but I should have seen this was going to happen. He couldn't handle the pressure.'

Leo was now, according to his mother, in a very private, very expensive clinic in Switzerland, leaving his country rudderless at a critical time. Leaving Mateo as the only one to step up and do his duty. To become King.

But Mateo had never been meant to be King.

Outside, the chapel bells of one of Cambridge's many colleges began to peal, a melodious sound so at odds with the bleak conversation he was having with his mother. His life was here, in the hallowed halls of this university, in the modern laboratories where he conducted important research into chemical processes and their effect on the climate.

He and his colleagues were on the brink of discovering how to neutralise certain chemical emissions and potentially reverse their effect on the climate. How could he leave it all behind, to become King of a country most people hadn't even heard about?

A country that was the linchpin in important economic talks, a country that was, if his mother was to be believed, on the brink of war.

'Mateo,' Agathe said softly, 'I know this is

hard. Your life has been in Cambridge. I understand that I am asking so much of you. Your country is.'

'You are not asking any more of me than you asked of my brothers,' Mateo said roughly. Agathe sighed.

'Yes, but they were prepared for it.'

And he wasn't. The implication was glaringly obvious. How could he be a good king, when he'd never been shown or taught? When no one had expected anything of him, except to live his own life as he pleased?

And he had done exactly that—going to Cambridge, becoming a lecturer and researcher, even living under a false name so no one knew he was a prince, eschewing the usual security and privileges to be his own man, free from all the encumbrances of royalty.

But all along he'd belonged to Kallyria.

'Mateo?' Agathe prompted and he gave a terse nod of acceptance.

'I'll fly back to Kallyria tonight.'

Agathe could not hide her relief; it shuddered through her with an audible sound. 'Thank you. Thank you.' Mateo nodded, knowing he was doing no more than his duty, even if it chafed bitterly. Of course he would still do it. There had never been any question of that.

'We must move quickly, to secure your throne,'

Agathe continued and Mateo stared at her, his blue-green eyes narrowed to aquamarine slits, his chiselled jaw bunched with tension.

'What do you mean?'

'Leo's abdication was so sudden, so unexpected. It has led to some…instability.'

'You mean from the insurgents?' A tribe of nomadic rabble, as far as he could tell, who hated any innovation or threat of modernity.

Agathe nodded, her forehead creased in worry. 'They are growing in power, Mateo, as well as number. Without anyone visible on the throne, who knows what they may do?'

Mateo's gut clenched at the thought of a war. It was so far from his experience, his *life*, that it was almost laughable. Tonight he was meant to be speaking at a fundraising dinner, followed by drinks with some university colleagues. Now those plans seemed ephemeral, ridiculous. He had a country to rule. A war to avoid, and if not, then win.

'I will do my best to put a stop to them,' he said, his tone assured and lethal. He might never have been meant to be King, but heaven knew he would step up to the role now. He would do whatever he had to secure his family, his country, his kingdom.

'I know you will,' Agathe assured him. 'But there is more, Mateo.' His mother looked hesitant, and Mateo frowned. What more could there be than what she had already said—his brother abdicating, his country on the verge of ruin, and the necessity for him to leave his entire life behind? How on earth could there be *more*?

'What do you mean?' he demanded. 'Mitera, what are you talking about?'

'Your rule must be made stable as quickly as possible,' Agathe explained. 'With your father and brothers…so much uncertainty…there must be no doubt, Mateo, that our line will rule. That our house will remain established, through all the foibles and fortunes of war.'

'I am travelling to Kallyria tonight,' Mateo answered, with an edge to his voice that he tried to moderate. His mother looked so worn down, so worried. He didn't want to hurt her or cause her any more concern. 'What else can I do?'

'You must marry,' Agathe told him bluntly. 'As quickly as possible, with an heir as soon as possible after that. I have drawn up a list of suitable brides…'

Mateo jerked upright, his mouth dropping open before he snapped it shut, his teeth grinding together. 'Marry? But Leo never married.' Six years his brother had been King, and he'd never even entertained the thought of a bride, as far as Mateo knew. There had certainly been no whispers of a potential match, never mind an engagement or a wedding. Leo had had numerous affairs with unsuitable women, many of them splashed across the tabloids, none of the fleeting relationships leading anywhere.

'It is different now,' Agathe said with bleak, regal honesty. 'There is no one else left.'

A bride.

He resisted the notion instinctively, with an elemental aversion both to marriage itself, and to marriage to a woman he didn't know or care about, a woman who would no doubt be so very *suitable.*

'And what women are on this list of brides?' he asked, a sardonic note entering his voice. 'As a matter of curiosity.'

'Admittedly, not very many. Your bride will play an important role, Mateo. She must be intelligent, not easily cowed, of the right birth and breeding…'

'So no vacuous socialites need apply?' Thank God. He could not stand the thought of being married to some grasping, faint-hearted miss who only wanted his money or title. Yet what kind of woman would agree to marry a man she'd never met? Not, Mateo suspected, one he wanted to share his life with.

'No, of course not.' Agathe gave him a severe look that reminded him of his childhood, of the days when he'd been unrepentantly unruly, testing all the boundaries to make sure they were there. 'You need a bride to suit your station, Mateo. A woman who will one day become Queen.' As she was. Yet no woman could match his mother for strength, elegance, or grace.

Mateo looked away. He couldn't bear to think about any of it. 'So who is on the list?' he asked after a moment.

'Vanessa de Cruz…a Spanish socialite who has started her own business. Women's wear.'

He made a scoffing sound. 'Why would she want to give all that up and become Queen?'

'You're a catch, Mateo,' Agathe said, a hint of a smile in her voice, despite all her sadness.

'She doesn't even know me,' he dismissed. He did not want to marry a woman who would only marry him for his title, her station in life. 'Who else?'

'A French heiress…a Turkish daughter of a CEO…in today's modern world, you need a woman who is her own person by your side. Not a princess simply waiting for the limelight.' His mother reeled off a few more names Mateo had barely heard of. Strangers, women he had no interest in knowing, much less marrying. He'd never intended to marry at all, and he certainly didn't want to love the woman whom he did, but neither did he want such a soulless arrangement as this.

'Think about it,' Agathe pressed gently. 'We can discuss it more when you arrive tonight.'

Mateo nodded his terse agreement, and a few minutes later he ended the video call. Outside the bells had stopped ringing. Mateo looked around his cluttered study, the research paper he'd been writing discarded on his desk, and accepted that his entire life had changed for ever.

'Something's come up.'

Rachel Lewis looked up from the microscope she'd been bending over to smile a greeting at her closest colleague. Mateo Karras' dazzlingly good looks had stopped stealing her breath years ago, thank goodness, but the academic part of her brain still couldn't help but admire the perfect symmetry of his features every time she saw him—the close-cropped blue-black hair, the aquamarine eyes the exact colour of the Aegean when she'd gone on holiday there a few years ago, the straight nose and square jaw, and of course the lithe and tall powerful figure encased now in battered cords and a creased button-down shirt, his usual work attire.

'Come up?' She wrinkled her nose, noting his rather terse tone, so unlike his usual cheerful briskness as he came into the lab, eager to get started. 'What do you mean?'

'I...' He shook his head, let out a weary breath.

'I'm going to be away for…a while. I'll have to take a leave of absence.'

'A leave of absence?' Rachel stared at him in shock. She and Mateo had been pioneering research on chemical emissions and climate change for the better part of a decade, since they'd both received their PhDs here at Cambridge. They were close, *so* close, to discovering and publishing the crucial evidence that would reduce toxic chemicals' effect on the climate. How could he be walking away from it all? It was too incredible to take in. 'I don't understand.'

'I know. I can't explain it all now. I'm afraid I have a family emergency that has to be dealt with. I… I don't know when I'll be back.'

'But…' Shock was giving way to dismay, and something even deeper that Rachel didn't want to consider too closely. She didn't *feel* anything for Mateo, not like that. It was just that she couldn't imagine working without him. They'd been colleagues and partners in research for so long, they practically knew each other's thoughts without needing to speak. When discussing their research, they'd completed each other's sentences on many occasions, with wry smiles and a rueful laugh.

They had a symmetry, a synchronicity, that had been formed over years of dedicated research, endless hours in the lab, as well as many drinks in pub gardens by the river Cam where they discussed everything from radioactive isotopes to organic compounds, and raced each other as to who could recite the periodic table the fastest. Unfortunately, Mateo always won. He *couldn't* be leaving.

'What's going on, Mateo? What's come up?' After nearly ten years together Rachel thought she surely deserved to know, even as she acknowledged that she and Mateo had shared next to nothing about their personal lives.

She didn't really have one, and Mateo had always been very private about his. She'd seen a few women on his arm over the years, but they hadn't stayed there very long—a date or two, nothing more. He'd never spoken about them, and she'd never dared ask.

She'd also never dared consider herself a candidate for that vaunted position—they were poles apart in terms of their appeal, and she was pragmatic enough to understand that, no matter how well they got along. Mateo would never, ever think of her that way. And, Rachel had reminded herself more than once with only a small pang of loss, it wasn't likely that any man would. She certainly hadn't found one yet, and she'd accepted her single state a long time ago, not that she'd ever admitted as much to Mateo.

Over countless conversations, they'd stuck to

chemistry, to research, maybe a bit of university gossip, but nothing more. Nothing personal. Certainly nothing *intimate*. And that had been fine, because their work banter was fun, their research was important, and being with Mateo made her happy.

Yet now Rachel knew she needed to know why he was leaving. Surely he couldn't walk away from it all without giving her a real reason.

'It's difficult to explain,' he said, rubbing a hand wearily over his face. Gone was his easy charm, his wry banter, the glint in his aquamarine eyes that Rachel loved. He looked remote, stony, almost like someone she didn't even know. 'All I can say is, it's a family emergency...'

Rachel realised she didn't know anything about his family. In nearly ten years, he'd never mentioned them once. 'I hope everyone is okay,' she said, feeling as if she were fumbling in the dark. She didn't even know if there was an *everyone*.

'Yes, yes, it will be fine. But...' He paused, and a look of such naked desolation passed over his face that Rachel had the insane urge to go over and give him a hug. Insane, because in nearly ten years she had never touched him, save for a brush of the shoulder as they leaned over a microscope together, or the occasional high five when they had a breakthrough in their research. But they'd never *hugged*. Not even close. It hadn't bothered or even occurred to her, until now.

'Let me know if there's something I can do to help,' she said. 'Anything at all. Are you leaving Cambridge…? Do you need your house looked after?' Although she'd never been to his house, she knew it was a sprawling cottage in the nearby village of Grantchester, a far cry from the terraced garden flat by the railway station that she'd scraped and saved to afford and make a cosy, comfortable home.

'I'm leaving the country.' Mateo spoke flatly. 'And I don't know when I'll be back.'

Rachel gaped at him. 'This sounds really serious, then.'

'It is.'

It also sounded so *final*. 'But you will come back?' Rachel asked. She couldn't imagine him not returning *ever*. 'When it's all sorted?' Whatever it was. 'I can't do this without you, Mateo.' She gestured to the microscope she'd been looking through, encompassing all the research they'd embarked on together, and a look of sadness and regret flashed across Mateo's face like a lightning strike of emotion, before his features ironed out and he offered her a nod.

'I know. I feel the same. I'm sorry.'

'Are you sure there isn't something I can do? Help in some way?' She didn't know what to do, how to help, and she hated that. She wanted to be useful, had spent her entire life trying to be necessary to people, if not actually loved. But Mateo was already shaking his head.

'No, no. You…you've been amazing, Rachel. A great colleague. The best I could ask for.'

She grimaced, struggling to make a joke of it even as horror stole over her at the thought of him leaving in such a final way. 'Don't, you make it sound as if you're dying.'

'It feels a little bit that way.'

'Mateo—'

'No, no, I'm being melodramatic.' He forced a smile to that mobile mouth that had once fascinated Rachel far more than it should have. Thankfully she'd got over that years ago. She'd made herself, because she'd known there was no point. 'Sorry, it's all just been a shock. I'll try to explain when I can. In the meantime…take care of yourself.'

He stepped forward then, and did something Rachel had never, ever expected him to do, although she'd dreamed it more times than she cared to admit. He leant forward and brushed her cheek with his lips. Rachel drew in a shocked breath as the sheer physicality of him assaulted her senses—the clean, citrusy smell of his aftershave, the softness of his lips, the sharp brush of his stubbled cheek against hers. One hand reached out, flailing towards him, looking for purchase, but thankfully her mind hadn't short-circuited quite that much, and she let it fall to her side before she actually touched him.

With a sad, wry smile, Mateo met her gaze and then stepped back. He nodded once more while Rachel stared dumbly, her mind spinning, her cheek buzzing, and then he turned around and left the lab. A second later Rachel heard the door to the block of laboratories close, and she knew he was gone.

CHAPTER TWO

MATEO STARED OUT at the idyllic view of his island home—sparkling sea, pure white beach, and the lovely, landscaped gardens of the royal palace stretching down to the sand, the flowers as bright as jewels amidst all the verdant green. A paradise, which he now knew was rotting at its core.

Everything was worse, far worse, than he'd thought. As soon as he'd arrived in Kallyria, he'd had briefings from all of his cabinet ministers, only to discover that Leo had been running the country—*his* country—into the ground. The economy, the foreign policy, even the domestic affairs that should have ticked over fairly smoothly had suffered under his brother's wildly unstable hand, with decisions being made recklessly, others carelessly reversed, world leaders insulted…the list went on and on, as his brother pursued pleasure and took an interest in affairs only when it suited him.

Mateo didn't know whether to be furious or

insulted that no one had informed him what was happening, and had been going on for years. As it was, all he felt was guilt. He should have known. He should have been here.

But then, no one had expected him to be. Certainly no one had ever asked. He turned from the window to glance down at the desk in the palace's study, a room that still reminded him of his father, with its wood-panelled walls and faint, lingering smell of cigar smoke—unless he was imagining that? His father had been gone for six years. Yet the room bore far more of an imprint of him than of Leo, who had, Mateo had discovered, spent more time on his yacht or in Monte Carlo than here, managing the affairs of his country.

Mateo's narrowed gazed scanned the list his mother had written out in her copperplate handwriting—the list of prospective brides. His mouth twisted in distaste at the mercenary nature of the venture; it seemed incredible to him that in this day and age, in a country that professed to be both progressive and enlightened, he was meant to marry a woman he didn't even know.

'Of course, you will get to know her, in time,' Agathe had assured him that morning, a tentative smile curving her mouth, lines of tension bracketing her eyes.

'And then impregnate her as quickly as possible?' Mateo queried sardonically. '*That's* not a recipe for disaster.'

'Arranged marriages can be successful,' his mother stated with quiet dignity. She should know; her own marriage had been arranged, and she'd striven tirelessly to make it work. Mateo knew his father had been a proud and sometimes difficult man; he'd had a great capacity for love and generosity, but also for anger and scorn. Mateo loved his mother; he'd admired his father. But he didn't want to emulate their marriage.

'I know they can, Mitera,' he said with a conciliatory smile, as he raked his hand through his hair. He'd arrived on Kallyria at ten o'clock last night, and only snatched an hour or two of sleep as he'd gone through all the paperwork his brother had left behind, and attended one debriefing meeting after another.

'Is it love you're looking for?' Agathe asked tentatively. 'Because love can grow, Mateo…'

'I don't want *love*.' He spoke the word with a sneer, because he had to. How else was he meant to think of it? 'I've already been in love, and I have no desire to be so again.'

'You mean Cressida.' Mateo didn't bother to reply. Of course he meant Cressida. 'That was a long time ago, Mateo.'

'I know.' He tried not to speak sharply, but he never talked about Cress. Ever. He tried not even to think about her, about the grief and guilt he still felt, like bullets embedded under his skin, a knife sticking out of his back that he couldn't twist around enough to pull out. If he didn't think about it, he didn't feel it, and that was his preferred way of managing the pain.

Agathe was silent for a moment, her hands folded in her lap, her head tilted to one side as she pinned Mateo in place with her perceptive gaze. 'Considering your aversion to that happy state, then, I would think an arranged marriage would suit you.'

Mateo knew she was right, and yet he still resisted the unpalatable notion. 'I want an agreement, not an arrangement,' he said after a moment. 'If I'm going to have my wife rule alongside me, bear and raise my children, be my partner in every way possible… I don't want to trust that role to a stranger who looks good on paper. That seems like the epitome of foolishness.'

'The women on this list have been vetted by several cabinet ministers,' Agathe countered. 'Everything about them is suitable. There is no reason to think they wouldn't be trustworthy, dutiful, admirable in every way.'

'And willing?' Mateo said with a curl of his lip. Agathe shook her head slowly.

'Why is that wrong?'

Mateo didn't answer, because he wasn't sure he

could explain it even to himself. All he knew was, after a lifetime of being told he would never be king, he didn't want a woman to marry him only because he finally was. But that felt too complicated and emotional to explain to his mother, and so he straightened his shoulders and reached for the piece of paper with its damned list.

'I'll look it over.'

Several hours later he was no closer to coming to a decision regarding any of the oh-so suitable candidates. He'd searched for information about them online, scanned their social media profiles, and found them all as duly admirable as his mother had insisted. One of his advisors had cautiously told him that initial overtures had been made, and at least four of the women had expressed their interest, despite knowing nothing about him. Having never spoken to him. Knowing only about his wealth and title, his power and prestige. Why did that bother him so much? Why did he *care*?

The whole point was, he didn't want to care. He wouldn't care. Yet he still hated the thought of it all.

His mobile buzzed and Mateo slid it out of his pocket. In the eighteen hours since he'd arrived on Kallyria he hadn't spoken to anyone from his former life, but now he saw with a ripple of undeniable pleasure that the call was from Rachel.

He swiped to take it. 'Yes?'

'Mateo?' She sounded uncertain.

'Yes, it's me.'

'You sounded so different there, for a second,' Rachel told him with an uncertain laugh. 'Like some… I don't know, some really important person.'

Mateo's lips twisted wryly. That was just what he'd become. Of course, he'd been important in his own way before returning to Kallyria; he held a fellow's chair at one of the world's most prestigious universities, and he'd started his own tech company as a side interest, and made millions in the process. Last year he'd been named one of Britain's most eligible bachelors by some ridiculous tabloid. But he hadn't been king.

'How are you?' Rachel asked. 'I've been worried about you.'

'Worried?' Mateo repeated shortly. 'Why?'

'Because you left so suddenly, for a family emergency,' Rachel said, sounding both defensive and a bit exasperated. 'Of course I'd be worried.'

'You needn't be concerned.' Too late Mateo realised how he sounded—brusque to the point of rudeness, and so unlike the usual way he related to his colleague. His *former* colleague. The truth was, he was feeling both raw and uncertain about everything, and he didn't want to admit that to anyone, not even Rachel.

Rachel. She'd been a good friend to him over the years, his closest friend in many ways although she knew little about his life, and he knew less about hers. They'd functioned on an academic plane, both enjoying the thrill of research, of making discoveries, of joking in the lab and discussing theories in the pub. Mateo didn't think he'd ever asked her about her personal life, or she about his. The thought had never occurred to him.

'I'm sorry,' he apologised, for his tone. 'But it's all under control.'

'Is it?' Rachel sounded hopeful. 'So you'll be back in Cambridge soon?'

Realisation thudded through Mateo at the assumption she'd so blithely made. The leave of absence he'd been granted was going to have to become a termination of employment, effective immediately, and yet he resisted the thought. Still, he steeled himself for what he knew had to be both said and done.

'No, I'm afraid I won't. I'm resigning from my position, Rachel.' He heard her soft gasp of surprised distress, and it touched him more than he expected it to. They might have been close colleagues, even friends, but Rachel would be fine without him. She'd find another research partner, maybe even move up in the department. It wasn't as if they'd actually *cared* about each other.

'But why?' she asked softly. 'What's going on, Mateo? Can't you tell me?'

He hesitated, then said, 'I need to take care of the family business. My brother was in charge but he's stepped down rather suddenly.'

'The family business...'

'Yes.' He wasn't ready to tell her the truth, that he was now king of a country. It sounded ridiculous, like something out of some soppy movie, and it made a lie of his life. Besides, she would find out soon enough. It would be in the newspapers, and rumours would ripple through the small, stifling university community. They always did.

'I can't believe it,' Rachel said slowly. 'You're really not coming back at all?'

'No.'

'And there's nothing I can do? No way I can help?'

'No. I'm sorry.' The words sounded so final, and Mateo knew there was no more to say. 'Goodbye, Rachel,' he said, and then he disconnected the call.

Rachel stared at her phone in disbelief. Had Mateo just *hung up* on her? Why was he acting as if he'd *died*?

And yet it felt as if he'd died. In truth, Rachel felt a far greater grief than she'd ever expected to, to have Mateo walk out of her life like that. She knew they hadn't actually been close in the way that most friends were, no matter how much they'd shared together. She suspected they wouldn't keep in touch. Mateo probably wouldn't even think of it. Typical scientist, existing on a mental plane rather than a physical one.

And yet Mateo Karras was a very physical man. Rachel had noticed it the moment she'd been introduced to him, when they'd both been obtaining their PhDs. Mateo had been in his third year while she'd been in her first, and the rumours had already been swirling around him, with the few female students in the department pretending to swoon whenever his name was mentioned.

Still, Rachel hadn't been prepared for the sheer physical presence of him, the base, animal attraction that had crashed over her, despite the glaring obviousness of their unsuitability. She was plain, nerdy, a little too curvy, with no fashion sense. Mateo might be a brilliant scientist, but he didn't fit the geeky stereotype as so many of his colleagues did.

He was devastatingly attractive, for a start, with close-cropped dark hair and those amazing blue-green eyes, plus a physique that could grace a calendar if he chose. He was also charming and assured, his easy manner and wry jokes disguising the fact that no one actually knew anything about him. Some people wondered at the aloofness under his easy exterior; some had called him a snob. Rachel had felt something else from him. Something like sadness.

In the intervening years, however, she'd disabused herself of that fanciful notion and accepted that Mateo was a man, and a law, unto himself. Charming and urbane, passionate about his work, he didn't need people the way most others did. The way Rachel had, and then learned not to, because it hurt less.

'Rachel? Is that you?' Her mother's wavery voice had Rachel slipping her phone into her pocket and plastering a smile on her face. The last thing she wanted to do was worry her mother about anything, not that she would even be worried. Or notice.

Carol Lewis had been diagnosed with Alzheimer's two years ago, and since then her decline had been dispiritingly steady. She'd moved into the second bedroom of Rachel's flat eighteen months ago. After living on her own since she was eighteen, Rachel had struggled to get used to her mother's company, as well as her many needs…and the fact that her mother had never actually seemed to *like* her very much. Neither of her parents had, and that had been something Rachel had made peace with, or thought she had.

Having her mother here tended to be an unwelcome reminder of the lack in their relationship.

'Hey, Mum.' Rachel smiled as her mother shuffled into the room, squinting at her suspiciously.

'Why were you making so much noise?'

She'd been talking quietly, but never mind. 'Sorry, I was on the phone.'

'Was it your father? Is he going to be late again?'

Her father had been dead for eight years. 'No, Mum, it was just a friend.' Although perhaps she couldn't call Mateo that any more. Perhaps she never could have called him that. 'Do you want to watch one of your shows, Mum?' Gently Rachel took her mother's arm and propelled her back to the bedroom, which had been kitted out with an adjustable bed and a large-screen TV. 'I think that bargain-hunter one might be on.' Since being diagnosed, her mother had developed an affinity for trashy TV, something that made Rachel both smile and feel sad. Before the disease, her mother had only watched documentaries, the obscurer and more intellectual the better. Now she gorged herself on talk shows and reality TV.

Carol let herself be settled back into her bed, still seeming grumpy as Rachel folded the blanket over her knees and turned on the TV. 'I could make you a toastie,' she suggested. 'Cheese and Marmite?'

Another aspect of the disease—her mother ate the same thing over and over again, for breakfast, lunch, and dinner. Rachel had gone through more jars of Marmite than she'd ever thought possible, especially considering that she didn't even like the stuff.

'All right,' Carol said, as if she were granting Rachel a favour. 'Fine.'

Alone in the kitchen, Rachel set to buttering bread and slicing cheese, Mateo's strangely brusque call weighing on her heavily. She was going to miss him. Maybe she shouldn't, but she knew she was. She already did.

Looking around the small kitchen—the tinny sound of the TV in the background, the uninspiring view of a tiny courtyard from her window—Rachel was struck with how *little* her life was.

She didn't go out. Her few friends in the department were married with children, existing in a separate, busy universe from her. Occasionally they invited her to what Rachel thought of as pity dinners, where they paraded their children in front of her and asked sympathetically if she wanted to be set up. Rachel could endure one of those about every six months, but she always left them with a huge sigh of relief.

The truth was, she hadn't felt the need or desire to go out, to have a social life, when she'd been working with Mateo for eight hours every day.

Their banter, their companionable silence, their occasional debates over drinks…all of it had been enough for her. More than enough, since she'd dealt with the stupid crush she'd had on him ages ago, like lancing a wound. Painful but necessary. Thank goodness she'd made herself get over that, otherwise she'd be in real trouble now.

'Rachel? Is my sandwich ready?'

With a sigh Rachel turned on the grill.

Three days later it was bucketing down rain as Rachel sprinted down the street towards her flat. She was utterly soaked, and even more dispirited by Mateo's disappearance from her life. She'd tried to be cheerful about gaining a new research partner, but the person put forward by the new chair was a smarmy colleague who liked to make disparaging comments about women and then hold his hands up, eyebrows raised, as he told her not to be so sensitive. Work had gone from being a joy to a disaster, and, considering the state of the rest of her life, that was a blow indeed.

She fumbled with the key to her flat, grateful that she'd have half an hour or so of peace and quiet before her mother came home. Carol spent her weekdays at a centre for the memory impaired, and was brought home by a kindly bus service run by the centre, which made Rachel's life a lot easier.

She was just pushing the door open when someone stepped out of the alleyway that led around to the back courtyard and the bins. Rachel let out a little scream at the sight of the figure looming out of the gloom and rain, yanking her key out of the door, ready to use it as an admittedly feeble weapon.

'Rachel, it's me.' The low thrum of his voice, with the faintest hint of an accent, had Rachel dropping her keys onto the concrete with a clatter.

'Mateo...?'

'Yes.' He took another step towards her and smiled. Rachel stared at him in wonder and disbelief.

'What are you doing here?'

'I wanted to see you.'

Rachel shook her head, sending raindrops splattering, too shocked even to think something coherent, much less say it. She realised just how glad she was to see him.

'May I come in? We're both getting soaked.'

'Yes, of course.' She scooped her keys up from the floor and pushed open the door. Mateo followed her into the flat, and as Rachel switched on the light she realised how small her flat probably seemed to him, and also that she had three ratty-looking bras drying over the radiator, and the remains of her jam-smeared toast on the coffee table, next to a romance novel with a cringingly lurid cover. Welcome to her life.

She turned to face Mateo, her eyes widening at the sight of him. He looked completely different, dressed in an expertly cut three-piece suit of dark grey, his jaw closely shaven, everything about him sleek and sophisticated and rich. He'd always emanated a certain assured confidence, but he was on another level entirely now. The disparity of their appearances—her hair was in rat's tails and she was wearing a baggy trouser suit with a mayonnaise stain on the lapel—made her cringe.

She shook her head slowly, still amazed he was in her flat. *Why?*

'Mateo,' she said questioningly, as if he might suddenly admit it wasn't really him. 'What are you doing here?'

CHAPTER THREE

THAT, MATEO REFLECTED, was a very good question. When the idea had come to him twenty-four hours ago, after his initial disastrous meeting with Vanessa de Cruz, it had seemed wonderfully obvious. Blindingly simple. Now he wasn't so sure.

'I wanted to see you,' he said, because that much was true.

'You did?' Rachel pushed her wet hair out of her eyes and gave him an incredulous look. 'Why?'

Another good question. In his mind's eye Mateo pictured Vanessa's narrowed gaze of avaricious speculation, the pouty pursing of her lips that he'd instinctively disliked. She'd been sleek and beautiful and so very cold.

'Of course we'll have a prenup,' she'd said.

He'd stiffened at that, even though he'd supposed it made sense.

'I believe marriage is for life.'

'Oh, no—you're not old-fashioned, are you?'

Mateo had never considered himself so before. In fact, he had always thought of himself as progressive, enlightened, at least by most standards. But when it came to marriage? To vows made between a man and a woman? Then, yes, apparently he was old-fashioned.

'Hold on,' Rachel said. 'I'm soaking wet and I think we could both use a cup of tea.' She shrugged off her sopping jacket, revealing a crumpled white blouse underneath that was becoming see-through from the damp, making Mateo uncomfortably aware of how generously endowed his former colleague was. He looked away, only to have his gaze fasten on some rather greying bras draped over the radiator.

Rachel tracked his gaze and then quickly swept them from the radiator, bundling them into a ball as she hurried into the kitchen. A few seconds later Mateo heard the distinctive clink of the kettle being filled and then switched on.

He shrugged off his cashmere overcoat and draped it over a chair at the small table taking up half of the cosy sitting room. The other half was taken up with a sofa covered in a colourful throw. He glanced around the flat, noting that, despite its smallness, it was a warm and welcoming place, with botanical prints on the walls and a tangle of house plants on the wide windowsill.

He scanned the titles in the bookcase, and then the pile of post on a marble-topped table by the front door. These little hints into Rachel's life, a life lived away from the chemistry lab, made him realise afresh that he didn't know anything about his former research partner.

Yes, you do. She worked hard and well for ten years. She can take a joke, but she knows what to take seriously. You've had fun with her, and, more importantly, you trust her.

Yes, he decided as he lowered himself onto the sofa, he knew enough.

The kettle switched off and a few minutes later Rachel came back into the sitting room with two cups of tea. She'd taken the opportunity to tidy herself up, putting her damp hair back in a ponytail, although curly tendrils had escaped to frame her face. She'd also changed her wet trouser suit for a heather-grey jumper that clung to her generous curves, and a pair of skinny jeans that showcased her just as curvy legs.

Mateo had never once looked at Rachel Lewis with anything remotely resembling sexual interest, yet now he supposed he ought to. At least, he ought to decide if he could.

'Here you are.' She handed him a cup of tea, black as he preferred, and then took her own, milky and sweet, and went to perch on the edge of an armchair that had a tottering pile of folded washing on it. 'Sorry for the mess,' she said with a wry grimace. 'If I'd known you were coming, I certainly wouldn't have left my bras out.'

'Or this?' He picked up the romance novel splayed out on the table, his lips quirking at the sight of the heaving bosom on the cover. '"Lady Arabella Fordham-Smythe is fascinated by the dark stranger who comes to her father's castle late one night..."'

'A girl's got to dream.' Humour glinted in her eyes again, reminding Mateo of how much fun she could be, although her cheeks had reddened a little in embarrassment. 'So why are you here, Mateo? Not that I'm not delighted to see you, of course.' Another rueful grimace, the glint in her eyes turning into a positive sparkle. 'Despite the lack of warning.'

'And the underwear.' *Why* were they talking about her underwear? Why was he imagining, not the worn-out bras she'd bundled away, but a slip in taupe silk, edged with ivory lace, one strap sliding from her shoulder...

The image jolted Mateo to the core, forcing him to straighten where he sat, and meet Rachel's laughing gaze once more.

Her eyes were quite lovely, he acknowledged. A deep, soft chocolate brown, with thick lashes fringing them, making her look like a gentle doe.

A doe with a good sense of humour and a terrific work ethic.

'Have you heard who has taken over as chair?' she asked, her grimace without any humour this time, and Mateo frowned.

'No. Who?'

'Supercilious Simon.' She made a face. 'I know I shouldn't call him that, but he is *so* irritating.'

Mateo's lip curled. 'That was the best they could do?' He was insulted that Simon Thayer, a mediocre researcher at best and a pompous ass to boot, had been selected to take his place.

'I know, I know.' Rachel shook her head as she blew on her tea. 'But he's always played the game. Cosied up to anyone important.' The sparkle in her eye had dimmed, and Mateo didn't like it. 'Working with him is going to be hell, frankly. I've even thought about going somewhere else, not that I could.' For a second she looked so desolate Mateo had a bizarre and discomfiting urge to comfort her. *How?* 'Anyway, never mind about that.' She shook her head, cheer resolutely restored. 'How are you? How is the family emergency?'

'Still in a state of emergency, but a bit better, I suppose.'

'Really?' Her eyes softened, if that were possible. Could eyes soften? Mateo felt uncomfortable just thinking about it. It was not the way he normally thought about eyes, or anyone. 'So why are you here, Mateo? Because you haven't actually said yet.'

'I know.' He took a sip of tea, mainly to stall for time, something he wasn't used to doing. When it came to chemistry, he was decisive. He knew what to do, no matter what the scientific conundrum. He saw a problem and he broke down the solution into steps, taking them one at a time, each one making sense.

So that was what he would have to do here. Take her through his reasoning, step by careful, analytical step. Rachel raised her eyebrows, a little smile playing about her generous mouth. Her lips, Mateo noticed irrelevantly, were rosy and lush.

And instead of starting at the beginning, and explaining it all coherently, he found himself doing the exact opposite—blurting out the end point, with no lead-up or context.

'I want you to marry me,' he said.

Rachel was sure she'd misheard. It had almost sounded as if Mateo had just asked her to marry him. In fact, that was *exactly* what it had sounded like, which couldn't be right. Obviously.

Unless he'd been joking…?

She gave him a quizzical little smile, as if she was unfazed, perhaps a bit nonplussed, rather than completely spinning inside and, worse, suddenly deathly afraid that he *was* joking. That it was so obviously a joke…as it had been once before. She'd been able to take it from Josh all those years ago, but she didn't think she could take it from Mateo, someone she both liked and trusted. *Please, please don't make me the butt of your joke.* 'Sorry,' she said lightly. 'Come again?'

'I didn't phrase that properly.'

Was there another way to phrase it? Rachel took a sip of her tea, mostly to hide her expression, which she feared was looking horribly hopeful. This was starting to feel like something out of the novel on the coffee table, and she knew, she *knew* real life wasn't like that. Mateo Karras did not want to marry her. No way. No how. It was impossible. Obviously.

'I want you to marry me,' he said again. 'But let me explain.'

'O…kay.'

'I'm not who you think I am.'

Now this was really beginning to seem melodramatic. Rachel had a sudden urge to laugh. 'Okay,' she said. 'Who are you?'

Mateo grimaced and put down his cup of tea. 'My full name and title? Prince Mateo Aegeus Karavitis, heir to the throne of the island kingdom of Kallyria.'

Rachel stared at him dumbly. He *had* to be joking. Mateo had liked to play a practical joke or two, back in the lab. Nothing serious or dangerous, but sometimes he'd relabel a test tube with some funny little slogan, and they had an ongoing contest of who could come up with the worst chemistry joke.

If H2O is the formula for water, what is the formula for ice? H2O cubed.

Was that what he was doing here? Was he making fun of her? Her cheeks stung with mortification at the thought, and her heart felt as if it were shrivelling inside her. Please, no…

'I'm sorry,' she said stiffly. 'I don't get it.'

Mateo frowned, the dark slashes of his brows drawing together. Why did he have to be so handsome? Rachel wondered irritably. It didn't make this any easier, or less painful. 'Get it?'

'The punchline,' she said flatly.

'There's no punchline, Rachel. I mean it. I accept this comes as a surprise, and it's not the most romantic proposal of marriage, but please let me explain.'

'Fine.' She put down her tea and folded her arms, feeling angry all of a sudden. If this was some long, drawn-out practical joke, it was in decided poor taste. 'Explain.'

Mateo looked a little startled by her hard tone, but he continued, 'Five days ago my brother Leo abdicated his throne.'

'Abdicated? He was King of this Kall—?'

'Kallyria, yes. He's been king for six years, since my father died.'

He spoke matter-of-factly and Rachel goggled at him. Was he actually serious? 'Mateo, why did you never say anything about this before? You're a *prince*—'

'I didn't say anything because I didn't want anyone to know. I wanted to succeed on my terms, as my own man. And that's exactly what I did. I used a different name, forewent any security protocols, and established myself on my own credentials.' His voice blazed with passion and purpose. 'No one at Cambridge knows who I truly am.'

'No one?'

'No one.'

For a terrible second Rachel wondered if Mateo was deluded somehow. It had happened before to scientists who spent too much time in the lab. They cracked. And the way he'd left so suddenly, this family emergency…what if it was all some weird delusion?

Her face crumpled in compassionate horror at the thought, and Mateo let out an exasperated breath. 'You don't believe me, do you?'

'It's not that…'

Mateo said something in Greek, most likely

a swear word. 'You think I'm actually making it up!'

'Not making it up,' Rachel soothed. 'I think you *believe* you're a prince…'

Mateo swore again, this time in English. He rose from her battered sofa in one fluid movement of lethal grace. 'Do I look or act like someone who is insane?' he demanded, and Rachel cringed a little.

No, he most definitely did not. In fact, with his eyes blazing blue-green fire, in a suit that looked as if it cost more than she made in a month, he *did* look like a prince. She sagged against the back of her chair, causing the pile of laundry to fall in a heap to the floor, as the realisation thudded through her.

'You really are a prince.'

'Of course I am. And in a week's time I am to be crowned king.'

He sounded so assured, so arrogant, that Rachel wondered how she could have doubted him for a minute. A second. And as for being deluded…of course he wasn't. She'd never seen a more sane, focused, determined individual in her life.

'But what does this have to do with me?' she asked shakily, as she remembered what he'd said. He wanted to *marry* her…

Surely not. *Surely not.*

'As King of Kallyria, I'll need a bride,' Mateo resumed his explanation as he paced the small confines of her sitting room. 'A queen by my side.'

Rachel shook her head slowly. She could not reconcile that statement with him wanting to marry her. Not in any way or form. 'Maybe I'm thick, Mateo, but I still don't understand.'

'You are not thick, Rachel.' He turned to face her. 'You are the smartest woman I know. A brilliant scientist, an incredibly hard worker, and a good friend.'

Her cheeks warmed and her eyes stung. He was speaking in a flat, matter-of-fact tone, but his words warmed her heart and touched her soul. She couldn't remember the last time she'd been given so much sincere praise.

'Thank you,' she whispered.

'I must marry immediately, to help stabilise my country. And produce an heir.'

Wait, what? Rachel stared at him blankly, still unable to take it in. She must be thick, no matter what Mateo had just said. 'And...and you want to marry *me*?' she asked in a disbelieving whisper. Even now she expected him to suddenly smile, laugh, and say of *course* it was a joke, and could she help him him to think of anyone suitable?

Yet she knew, just looking at him, that it wasn't. He'd come back to Cambridge; he'd come to her flat to find her. He looked deadly serious, incredibly intent.

Mateo Karras—no, Karavitis—Prince—no, *King* of a country—wanted to marry her. *Her.* When no man had ever truly wanted her before. Still, she felt uncertain. Doubtful. Josh's words, spoken over a decade before, still seared her brain and, worse, her heart.

How could any man want you?

'Why?' Rachel whispered. Mateo didn't pretend to misunderstand.

'Because I know you. I trust you. I *like* you. And we work well together.'

'In a chemistry lab—'

'Why not in a kingdom?' He shrugged. 'Why should it be any different?'

'But…' Rachel shook her head slowly '…you're not offering me the vice-presidency, Mateo. You're asking me to be your *wife*. There's a huge difference.'

'Not that much.' Mateo spread his hands. 'We'd be a partnership, a team. I'd need you by my side, supporting me, supporting my country. We'd be working together.'

'We'd be *married*.' An image slammed through her head, one she had no business thinking of. A wedding night, candles all around, the slide of burnished skin on skin…

Like something out of the book on the table.

No. That wasn't real. That wasn't her. And Mateo certainly didn't mean that kind of marriage.

Except he'd mentioned needing an heir. As soon as possible.

'Yes,' Mateo agreed evenly. 'We'd be married.'

Rachel stared at him helplessly. 'Mateo, this is crazy.'

'I know it's unexpected—'

'I have a *job*,' she emphasised, belatedly remembering the life she'd built for herself, just as Mateo had, on her own terms. She'd won her place first at Oxford and then Cambridge, and finally her research fellowship, all on her own merit, not as the daughter of esteemed physicist, William Lewis, with his society wife Carol. She'd made no mention of her parents in any of her applications, had made sure nobody knew. She'd wanted to prove herself, and she *had*.

And Mateo was now thinking she might leave it all behind, everything she'd worked so hard for, simply to be his trophy wife, a mannequin on his arm? She started to shake her head, but Mateo forestalled her, his voice calm and incisive.

'I realise I am asking you to sacrifice much. But you would have limitless opportunity as Queen of Kallyria—to promote girls' involvement in STEM subjects; to fund research and support charities and causes that align with your interests; to travel the world in the name of science.'

'Science? Or politics?' she asked, her voice shaking with the enormity of it all. She couldn't grasp what he was asking her on so many incredible levels.

'Both,' Mateo replied, unfazed. 'Naturally. As king, one of my priorities will be scientific research. Kallyria has a university in its capital city of Constanza. Admittedly, it is not on the same level as Cambridge or Oxford, but it is esteemed among Mediterranean countries.'

'I don't even know where Kallyria is,' Rachel admitted. 'I'm not sure I've ever heard of it before.'

'It is a small island country in the eastern Mediterranean Sea. It was settled by Greek and Turkish traders, over two thousand years ago. It has never been conquered.'

And he was asking her to be its *Queen*. Rachel felt as if her head were going to explode.

'I don't…' she began, not even sure what she was going to say. And then the front doorknob rattled, and her mother shuffled into the house, looking between her and Mateo with hostile suspicion.

'Rachel,' she demanded, her voice rising querulously. 'Who is this?'

CHAPTER FOUR

MATEO STARED DISPASSIONATELY at the old woman who was glaring back at him.

'Mum,' Rachel said faintly. 'This is...' She glanced uncertainly at Mateo, clearly not sure how to introduce him.

'My name is Mateo Karavitis,' Mateo intercepted smoothly as he stepped forward and offered his hand. 'A former colleague of your daughter's.'

Rachel's mother looked him up and down, seeming unimpressed. 'Why are you visiting here?' She turned back to Rachel. 'I'm hungry.'

'I'll make you a toastie,' Rachel said soothingly.

She threw Mateo a look that was half apology, half exasperation. He gave her an assured, blandly unfazed smile in return.

So Rachel had a mother who was clearly dependent on her care. It was a surprise, but it did not deter him. If anything, it offered her an added incentive to agree to his proposal, since he would be able to offer her mother top-of-the-line care, either here in England or back in Kallyria.

Not, Mateo reflected as Rachel hurried to the kitchen and her mother harrumphed her way to her bedroom, that she needed much incentive. Judging from everything he'd seen so far of her life outside work, there was nothing much compelling her to stay.

He fully anticipated, after Rachel had got over the sheer shock of it, that she'd agree to his proposal. How could she not?

He came over to stand in the doorway of the kitchen. Rachel was looking harassed, slicing cheese as fast as she could.

'How long has your mother been living with you?' he asked.

'About eighteen months.' She reached for a jar of Marmite and Mateo stepped forward.

'May I help?'

'What?' Rachel looked both frazzled and bewildered, her hair falling into her eyes. 'No—'

Deftly he unscrewed the jar of Marmite she seemed to have forgotten she was holding. Plucking the knife from her other hand, he began to spread the Marmite across the bread. 'Cheese and Marmite toastie, yes?'

'What?' She stared at him blankly, then down to the bread he was preparing. 'Oh. Er… Yes.'

Mateo finished making the sandwich and placed it on the hot grill. 'Shouldn't be a moment.'

'I don't understand,' Rachel said helplessly. Mateo arched an eyebrow.

'How to make a toastie? You did seem to be having trouble mastering the basics, but I was happy to step in.'

A smile twitched her lips, and Mateo realised how much he'd missed their banter. 'Thank goodness for capable males,' she quipped. 'What on earth would I have done if you hadn't been here?'

His lips quirked back a response. 'Heaven only knows.'

'I shudder to think. Careful it doesn't burn.' She nodded to the grill. 'I'll make my mother a cup of tea—do you want another one?'

'Not unless it has a generous splash of whisky in it.'

'Sorry, I'm afraid that's not possible. Not unless you want to nip out to the off-licence on the corner.'

He stepped closer to her. 'What I really want is to take you to dinner to discuss my proposal properly.'

A look of fear flashed across Rachel's face, surprising him. He didn't think he'd ever seen her actually look afraid before. 'Mateo, I don't think there's any point—'

'I think there is, and, considering how long we

have known each other, I also think it's fair to ask for an evening of your time. Assuming your mother can be left for a few hours?'

'As long as she's eaten and the TV's on,' Rachel answered with clear reluctance. 'I suppose.'

'Good. Then I will make arrangements.' He slid his phone out of his pocket and quickly thumbed a text to the security guard he had waiting outside in a hired sedan.

Smoke began to pour out of the oven. 'I think you've burned my mother's toastie,' Rachel said tartly, and with a wry grimace Mateo hurried to rescue the sandwich from the grill.

Half an hour later, Carol Lewis was settled in front of a lurid-looking programme, a toastie and cup of tea on her lap tray.

'I'll be back in about an hour, Mum,' Rachel said, sounding anxious. 'If you need anything, you can always knock on Jim's door.'

'Jim?' Carol demanded. 'Who's Jim?'

'Mr Fairley,' Rachel reminded her patiently. 'He lives in the flat upstairs, number two?' Her mother harrumphed and Rachel gave Mateo an apologetic look as she closed her bedroom door. 'Do I need to change?'

Mateo swept his glance over her figure, noting the way the soft grey cashmere clung to her breasts. 'You look fine.'

Her lips twisted at that, although Mateo wasn't

sure why, and she nodded. 'Fine. Let's get this over with.'

Not a promising start, but Mateo was more than hopeful. The more he saw of Rachel's life, the more he was sure she would agree…eventually.

Outside the drenching downpour had tapered off to a misty drizzle, and an autumnal breeze chilled the air. Rachel had shrugged on a navy duffel coat and a rainbow-colored scarf, and Mateo took her elbow as he led her to the waiting car.

'We're not walking?'

'I made a reservation at Cotto.'

'That posh place in the Gonville Hotel?' She pulled her arm away from him, appalled. 'It's so expensive. And I'm not dressed appropriately—'

'You'll be fine. And we're in a private room, anyway.'

She shook her head slowly, not looking impressed so much as uncertain. 'Who *are* you?'

'You know who I am.'

'You never did this before. Private rooms, hired cars—'

'I need to take necessary precautions for my privacy and security, as well as yours. Once it becomes known that I am the King of Kallyria—'

'I can't help but think you're deluded when you say that,' Rachel murmured.

Mateo allowed himself a small smile. 'I assure you, I am not.'

'I know, I really do believe you. I just…don't believe this situation.'

The driver hopped out to open the passenger door of the luxury sedan. Mateo gestured for Rachel to get in first, and she slid inside, running one hand over the sumptuous leather seats.

'Wow,' she murmured, and then turned to face the window.

Mateo slid in beside her, his thigh brushing hers. She moved away. He thought about pressing closer, just to see, but decided now was not the time. The physical side of their potential arrangement was something that would have to be negotiated carefully, and there were certainly other considerations to deal with first.

They didn't speak as the driver navigated Cambridge's traffic through the dark and rain, and finally pulled up in front of the elegant Georgian façade of the Gonville Hotel. A single snap of his fingers at the concierge had the man running towards him, and practically tripping over himself to accommodate such an illustrious personage as the Crown Prince, soon to be King.

Rachel stayed silent as they were ushered into a sumptuous private room, with wood-panelled walls and a mahogany table laid for two with the finest porcelain and silver.

'I've never seen you like this before,' she said once the concierge had closed the door behind them, after Mateo had dismissed him, not wanting to endure his fawning attentions any longer. She shrugged off her coat and slowly unwound her scarf.

'Seen me like what?' Mateo pulled out her chair and she sat down with murmured thanks.

'Acting like...like a king, I suppose. Like you own the place. I mean, you were always a little *arrogant*,' she conceded as she rested her chin in her hand, 'but I thought it was just about your brain.'

Mateo huffed a laugh. 'I'm wondering if I should be offended by that.'

'No, you shouldn't be. I'm basically telling you you're smart.'

'Well, then.'

'Except,' Rachel continued, 'I don't think you're making a very smart decision here.'

Mateo's gaze narrowed as he flicked an uninterested glance at the menu. 'Oh?'

'No, I don't. Really, Mateo, I'd make a terrible queen.'

Rachel eyed him mischievously, her chin still in her hand. It was actually a bit amusing, to see this self-assured man, who was kind of scaring her in his fancy suit, look so discomfited. It helped her take her mind off the fact that he'd asked her to marry him, and she still had absolutely no idea how to feel about that. Flattered? Furious? Afraid? Appalled? All four, and more.

'I disagree with that assessment,' Mateo said calmly.

'I can't imagine why.'

He frowned, and even when he was looking so ferocious, Rachel couldn't help but acknowledge how devastatingly handsome he was. The crisp white shirt and cobalt-blue tie were the perfect foil for his olive skin and bright blue-green eyes. He'd looked amazing in rumpled shirts and old cords; he looked unbelievably, mouth-dryingly gorgeous now. And it was yet another reminder that they couldn't possibly marry each other.

'I don't understand why you are putting yourself down,' he said, and Rachel squirmed a bit at that. It made her feel pathetic, and she wasn't. A long time ago she'd accepted who she was…and who she wasn't. And she'd been okay with that. She'd made herself be okay, despite the hurt, the lack of self-confidence, the deliberate decision to take potential romance out of the equation of her life.

On the plus side, she had a good brain, a job she loved—or at least she'd *had*—and she had a few good friends, who admittedly had moved on in life in a way she hadn't, but *still*. She'd taken stock of herself and her life and had decided it was all good.

'I'm not putting myself down. I'm just being realistic.'

'Realistic?' Mateo's dark eyebrows rose, his eyes narrowed in aquamarine assessment. 'About not being a good queen? How would you even know?'

'I'm terrible at public speaking.' It was the first thing she could think of, even though it had so little to do with her argument it was laughable.

Mateo's eyebrows rose further. 'You are not. I have heard you deliver research papers to a full auditorium on many occasions.'

'Yes, but that was research. Chemistry.'

'So?'

She sighed, wondering why she was continuing this ridiculous line of discussion, even as she recognised it was safer than many others. 'I can talk about chemistry. But other things…'

'Because you are passionate about it,' Mateo agreed with a swift nod. Rachel felt her face go pink at the word passionate, which was embarrassing. He wasn't talking about passion in *that* way, and in any case she couldn't think about that aspect of a marriage between them without feeling as if she might scream—or self-combust. 'So you will have to find other things you are passionate about,' he continued calmly. 'I am sure there are many.'

Now her face was fiery, which was ridiculous. Rachel snatched up her menu. 'Why don't we order?'

'I have already ordered. The menu is simply so you can see their offerings.'

'You ordered for me?' Her feminist principles prickled instinctively.

Mateo gave a small smile. 'Only to save on time, since I know you are concerned about your mother, and also because I know what you like.'

'I've never even been to the restaurant.' Now she was a bit insulted, which was easier than feeling all the other emotions jostling for space in her head and heart.

'All right.' Mateo leaned back in his chair, his arms folded, a cat-like smile curling his mobile mouth. A mouth she seemed to have trouble looking away from. 'Look at the menu and tell me what you would order.'

'Why? It's too late—'

'Humour me. And be honest, because if you order the black truffle and parmesan soufflé, I'll know you're lying. You hate truffles.'

How did he know that?

One of their seemingly innocuous conversations in the lab or the pub, Rachel supposed. They might not have shared the intimate details of their personal lives, but food likes and dislikes had always been a safe subject for discussion.

She glanced down at the menu, feeling self-conscious and weirdly exposed, even though they were just talking about choices at a restaurant. Across the table Mateo lounged back in his chair, that small smile playing about his lips, looking supremely confident. He was so sure he knew what she was going to order.

Rachel continued to peruse the offerings, tempted to pick something unlikely, yet knowing Mateo would see through such a silly ploy.

'Fine.' She put the menu down and gave him a knowing look. 'The beetroot and goat cheese salad to start, and the asparagus risotto for my main.'

His smile widened slightly as his gaze fastened on hers, making little lightning bolts run up and down her arms. Now, *that* was alarming. She'd inoculated herself against Mateo's obvious attraction years ago. She'd had to.

You couldn't work with someone day in and day out, heads bent close together, and feel sparkly inside while the person next to you so obviously felt nothing. It was positively soul-deadening, not to mention ego-destroying, and Rachel had had enough of both of those. And so she'd made herself not respond to him, not even *think* about responding to him.

Yet now she was.

'So is that what you ordered for me?' she asked, a little bolshily, to hide her discomfort and awareness.

'Let's find out, shall we?' As if on cue, a waiter came quietly into the private room, two silver-domed dishes in his hands. He set them at their places, and then lifted the lids with a flourish. Rachel stared down at her beetroot and goat cheese salad and felt ridiculously annoyed.

'You just like winning,' she told him as she took her fork. The salad did look delicious. 'I mean, how many hours did you practise reciting the periodic table just to beat me?'

'Practise,' Mateo scoffed. 'As if.'

She shook her head slowly as she toyed with a curly piece of radicchio. 'You might know what I like to eat, but that's all.'

'All?'

'That is not a challenge. I just mean…we don't actually know each other, Mateo.' She swallowed, uncomfortably aware of the throb of feeling in her voice. 'I know we've worked together for ten years, and we could call each other friends, but… I didn't even know you were a prince.'

'No one knew I was a prince.'

'And you don't know anything about me. We've never really talked about our personal lives.'

She felt a ripple of frustration from Mateo,

like a wavelength in the air. He shrugged as he stabbed a delicate slice of carpaccio on his plate. 'So talk. Tell me whatever it is you wish me to know.'

'What an inviting prospect. Why don't I just give you my CV?'

'I've seen your CV, but do feel free.'

Rachel shook her head. 'It's not just a matter of processing some information, Mateo. It's *why* we don't know anything about each other. Ten years working together, and you don't even know…' she cast about for a salient fact '…my middle name.'

'Anne,' Mateo answered immediately. And at her blank look, 'It's on your CV.'

Rachel rolled her eyes. 'Fine, something else, then. Something that's not on my CV.'

Mateo cocked his head, his gaze sweeping slowly over her, warming everywhere it touched, as if she were bathed in sunlight. 'I'm not going to know something you haven't told me,' he said after a moment. 'So it's pointless to play a guessing game. But I know more about you than perhaps you realise.'

Which was a very uncomfortable thought. Rachel squirmed in her seat at the thought of how much Mateo could divine from having worked so closely with her for ten years. All her quirks, idiosyncrasies, annoyances… She really did not want to have the excoriating experience of having him list everything he'd noticed over the past decade.

He was a scientist, trained in matters of observation. He would have noticed *a lot*, and she should have noticed the same amount about him, but the trouble was she'd been exerting so much energy trying *not* to notice him that she wasn't sure she had.

Which put him at a distinct and disturbing advantage.

'Look, that isn't really the point,' she said quickly. 'This is not even about you knowing or not knowing me.'

'Is it not? Then what is it about?'

Rachel stared at him helplessly. She wasn't going to say it. She wasn't going to humiliate herself by pointing out the glaringly obvious discrepancies in their stations in life, in their *looks*. She didn't want to enumerate in how many ways she was not his equal, how absurd the idea of a marriage between them would seem, because she'd been in this position before and it had been the worst experience of her life.

'It's about the fact that I don't want to marry you,' she said in as flat and final a tone as she could. 'And I certainly don't want to be queen of a country.'

Something flickered across Mateo's beautiful face and then was gone. His gaze remained steady on hers as he answered. 'While I will naturally accept your decision if that is truly how you feel, I do not believe you have given it proper consideration.'

'That's because it is so outrageous—'

He leaned forward, eyes glinting, mouth curved, everything in him alert and aware and somehow predatory. Rachel tried not to shrink back in her seat. She'd never seen Mateo look so intent.

'I think,' he said, 'it is my turn to give my arguments.'

CHAPTER FIVE

RACHEL'S EYES WIDENED at his pronouncement, lush lashes framing their dark softness in a way that made Mateo want to reach across the table and touch her. Cup her cheek and see if her skin was as soft as it looked. He realised he hadn't actually *touched* his former colleague very much over the last ten years. Brushed shoulders, perhaps, but not much more. But that was something to explore later.

Right now she needed convincing, and he was more than ready to begin. He'd patiently listened to her paltry arguments, sensing that she wasn't saying what she really felt. What she really feared. And he'd get to that in time, but now it was his turn to explain why this was such a very good idea.

Because, after an evening in her presence, Mateo was more convinced than ever that it was. Rachel was smart and focused and, more importantly, he *liked* her. And best of all, he *only* liked her. While he sensed a spark of attraction for her that could surely be fanned into an acceptable flame, he knew he didn't feel anything more than that.

No overwhelming emotion, no flood of longing, desire, or something deeper. And if he didn't feel that after ten years basically by her side, he would never feel it.

Which was a very good thing.

'All right,' Rachel said, her voice wavering slightly although her gaze was sharp and focused, her arms folded. 'I'm waiting for these brilliant arguments.'

'I didn't say they were brilliant,' Mateo replied with a small smile. 'But of course they are.'

Rachel rolled her eyes. 'Of course.'

Mateo paused, enjoying their back and forth as he considered how best to approach the subject. 'The real question, I suppose,' he said slowly, 'is why *wouldn't* we get married?' He let that notion hover in the air between them, before it landed with a thud.

'Why wouldn't we?' Rachel repeated disbelievingly. 'Please, Mateo. You're a *scientist*. Don't give me an argument from fallacy. Neither of us is married. Therefore we should marry. That is *not* how it works.'

'That is not how science works,' Mateo agreed, hiding his smile at her response. She was so fiery.

He'd never enjoyed it quite so much before. 'But this isn't science.'

'Isn't it?' she challenged, a gleam in her eye that looked a little too much like vulnerability. 'Because I'm not sure what else it could be.'

She had him on the back foot, and he didn't enjoy the sensation. Mateo took a sip of the wine the waiter had brought—a Rioja because he knew Rachel liked fruity reds—to stall for time. 'Elucidate, please.'

'Fine, I'll *elucidate.*' She lifted her chin slightly, her eyes still gleaming, making Mateo feel even more uncomfortable. Something more was going on here than what was apparent, and it made him a little nervous. 'You came back to Cambridge to convince me to marry you. Considering we've never dated or even thought about dating for an entire decade, it's hardly love or physical attraction that brought you to my doorstep.' She spoke matter-of-factly, which was a relief. He must have been imagining that unnerving note of vulnerability in her voice, of something close to hurt. Yes, he had to have been.

'True,' Mateo was willing to concede with a brief nod.

'So the reasons for wanting me to marry you are scientific, or at least expedient, ones. Let me guess.' She paused, and Mateo almost interrupted her. He wasn't sure he wanted his arguments framed in her perspective.

'All right,' he said after a moment, leaning back in his chair to make it seem as if he were more relaxed than he was. 'Guess.'

Rachel pursed her lips, her gaze becoming distant as she considered. Mateo waited, feeling tense, expectant, almost eager now to hear what she thought.

'We get along,' she said at last. 'We have a fairly good rapport, which I imagine would be important if we were working together to rule a country.' She shook her head, smiling ruefully. 'I can't believe I'm even *saying* that.'

'I take exception to *fairly*,' Mateo interjected with a small smile, willing her to smile back. She did, tightly.

'Fine. We get along well. Very well, even.'

He inclined his head. 'Thank you.'

Rachel let out a breath. 'And we know each other, on a basic level.'

'More than a basic—'

'You said you trust me,' she cut across him.

'I do.' His heartfelt words seemed to reverberate between them, and Mateo watched with interest as her cheeks went pink.

'Still,' Rachel pressed. 'None of that is reason to get married.'

Mateo arched an eyebrow. 'Is it not?'

'If it was, you should have asked Leonore Worth to marry you,' she flung at him a bit tartly.

'Leonore?' She was a lecturer in biology at the university, a pointy woman with a nasal laugh whom he'd escorted to a department function once. He hadn't made that mistake again. But why was Rachel mentioning *her*? 'Why would I do that?' he asked.

'Because she's…' Rachel paused, drawing a hitched breath. Her cheeks were turning red. 'More suited to the role than I am,' she finished.

Mateo stared at her, mystified. 'I am wondering, from a purely scientific view, of course, how you arrived at that conclusion.'

She shook her head, looking tired, even angry. 'Come on, Mateo,' she said in a low voice. 'Stop it.'

'Stop what?'

'Pretending you don't know what I'm talking about.'

'I don't.' Of that he was sure. They were skirting around something big and dark but damned if he knew what it was.

Rachel flung her arms out, nearly knocking her plate of almost untouched salad to the floor. 'I am not queen material.'

'Define your terms, please,' Mateo said. Perhaps it would be easier if they did make this as scientific as possible: What is queen material?

'Oh, this is pointless,' she cried. 'I'm not going to marry you. I'm not going to leave my job—'

'Toadying up to smarmy Simon?' he interjected. 'You've already said you're considering looking elsewhere.'

'I didn't really mean that.'

'Your job has changed, Rachel, and not for the better. I'm offering you a greater opportunity.'

'To hang on your arm?' Her sneer was insulting.

'Of course not. If I wanted a mere trophy wife, I would have picked one of the eminently suitable candidates on the list my mother drew up.'

Rachel nearly choked at that, her soft brown eyes going shocked and wide. 'There's a list?'

'Yes, more's the pity. I don't want a trophy wife, one who ticks all the boxes. I want someone I can trust. Someone who makes me laugh. Someone who, dare I sound so sentimental, *gets* me.'

Tears filled her eyes, appalling him. He'd been trying for humour, but he feared he'd only sounded twee. 'Rachel…'

'Why are you making this so hard?' she whispered, blinking back tears. Her teeth sank into her lower lip, creating two rosy indents he had the urge to soothe away—with his tongue. Mateo forced the unwanted and unhelpful image back.

'I'm making it hard because I want you to agree.'

'And if I did?'

The thrill of victory raced through his veins, roared in his ears. Never mind that she sounded a bit sad, a touch defeated. *She was actually considering it.*

'Then I'd arrange for you to travel back to Kallyria with me as soon as possible. We'd be married as soon as possible after that, in the Cathedral of Saint Theodora. Everyone in the royal family has been married in the Greek Orthodox church. I hope that is acceptable to you.'

'Mateo, I was speaking hypothetically.'

He shrugged, refusing to be deterred. 'So was I.'

'But after the ceremony? What then?'

'Then we live together as man and wife. You accompany me to state functions, on royal tours. You decide on which charitable institutions you wish to pioneer or support.'

'And I give you an heir?' She met his gaze even though her cheeks were fiery now. 'That's a part of this marriage deal you haven't actually mentioned yet.'

'No, I haven't,' Mateo agreed after a moment. He wished he knew why she was blushing—was it just because they were talking about sex?

Or was it something else, something more? 'It seemed fairly obvious.'

'That this would be a marriage in…in every sense of the word?'

'If, by that phrase, you mean we'd consummate it, then yes.' He held her gaze evenly despite the images dancing through his mind. Images he'd never, ever indulged in before, of Rachel in slips of silk and lace, smiling up at him from a canopied bed in the royal palace, her thick, wavy hair spread across the pillow in a chocolate river…

'Don't you think that's kind of a big thing to discuss?' Rachel asked, her voice sounding a little strangled. 'Obvious as it may seem?'

'Fine.' Mateo spread his hands as a waiter came in to quickly and quietly clear their dishes. 'Then let's discuss it.'

What had she got herself into? Rachel sat in silent mortification, willing her blush to recede, as the waiter cleared their plates and Mateo waited, completely unfazed by the turn in the conversation, just as he'd been unfazed by everything that had already been said.

He was like a bulldozer, flattening her every objection, making his proposal seem obvious, as if she should have been expecting it. And meanwhile Rachel felt as if she kept stumbling down rabbit holes and across minefields, dodging all the dangers and pitfalls, as she was accosted by yet another reason why a marriage between them would never work.

'You're not attracted to me,' she stated baldly. It hurt to say it; it humiliated her beyond all measure, in fact, and brought up too many bad memories or, really, just one in particular, but Rachel had long ago realised that confronting the elephant in the room, naming and shaming it, was the only way forward for her dignity. She'd done it before and she'd do it again, and she'd come out stronger for it. That much had been her promise to herself, made when she was a shy and naïve twenty and still holding true today, twelve years later.

She held his gaze and watched his lips purse as an expression flickered across his face that she would have given her eye teeth to identify, but could not.

'Sexual attraction is not a strong foundation for a marriage,' he said at last, and Rachel swallowed, trying not to let the sting of those words penetrate too deeply.

'It's not the most important part, perhaps,' she allowed. 'But it matters.'

Another lengthy silence, which told her just how unattracted to her he had to be. Rachel took a sip of wine, her gaze lowered, as she did her best to keep Mateo from knowing how much he was hurting her.

'I don't believe it will be an obstacle to our state of matrimony,' he said at last. 'Unless you have an intense aversion to me?' He said this with such smiling, smug self-assurance that Rachel had the sudden urge to throw her wine in his face. Oh, no, of *course* it couldn't be the case that she found him undesirable. Of course *that* was a joke.

'It might surprise you,' she said with a decided edge to her voice, 'but I want more from a potential marriage than the idea that my attractiveness, or lack of it, won't be an *obstacle*.'

Mateo's eyes widened as he acknowledged her tone, the rise and fall of her chest. She saw his lips compress and his pupils flare and knew he didn't like her sudden display of emotion. Well, she didn't like it, either.

She was far too agitated for either of their own good, and their reasonable, scientific discussion had morphed into something emotional and, well, *awful*. Because she really didn't want any more explanations about how he was willing to sacrifice sexual attraction on the altar of—what? His duty? Their compatibility? Logic? Whatever it was, Rachel didn't want to know. She'd had enough of being patronised. Enough of being felt as if she'd just about do. She'd had enough of that before this absurd conversation had even begun.

'Please.' She raised one hand to forestall any explanations he might have felt compelled to give, throwing her napkin onto the table with the other. 'Please don't say anything more, because I really don't want to hear it. Any of it. I am not going to marry you, Mateo, end of. Thanks anyway.'

She rose from the table on unsteady legs, her chest still heaving. She had to get out of here before she did something truly terrible, like start to cry.

But before she could even grab her coat, Mateo had risen from his own seat and crossed the small table to take her by the arms, his grip firm and sure.

'If you will not believe my words,' he said in a voice bordering a growl, 'then perhaps you will believe my actions.'

And then he kissed her.

It had been a long time since Rachel had been kissed. So long, in fact, that she'd sort of forgotten she had lips. Lips that could be touched and explored and licked. Lips that Mateo was moving over with his own, his tongue tracing the seam of her mouth before delving inward, making her knees weaken. She'd never known knees to actually do that before. She'd considered it a metaphor rather than scientific fact.

His lips felt both hard and soft, warm and cool. A thousand sensations exploded inside her as she parted her own lips, inviting him in. He reached up and cupped her cheek with his big, warm hand, his thumb stroking her skin, making her both shiver and shudder. Everything felt as if it were on fire.

The kiss went on and on, deeper and deeper, fireworks exploding all over her body. She'd never been kissed like this. She'd never *felt* like this.

Her hands came up of their own accord to clutch at his hard shoulders, fingers clawing at him, begging him for more.

And he gave it, one knee sliding between her own willing legs, the length of his hard, taut body pressed against hers for one glorious second before he stepped away, looking as composed to Rachel's dazed gaze as if they'd just shaken hands.

While she…she was in pieces. *Pieces*, scattered on the floor, with her mind spinning too much to even start to pick them up.

'I think that proves,' Mateo said in a clipped voice as he straightened his suit jacket, 'that attraction is not an issue.'

He stood there, a faint smile curling his mouth, his eyes gleaming with unmistakable triumph, while Rachel was still gasping and reeling from what had obviously been an unremarkable kiss to him. Meanwhile it had rocked her world right off its axis. Heaven only knew if she'd be able to straighten it again.

Standing in front of her, his arms folded, his eyebrows raised, he looked so confident, so utterly assured of his undeniable masculine appeal, that Rachel wanted to scream. Claw the face she'd just kissed. Had he really felt it necessary to prove how in thrall to him she could be?

While he seemed almost at pains to show how utterly unaffected he was—his expression composed, his breathing even, his manner bland.

Damn him.

'If you thought that was meant to win me over, you were wrong,' Rachel choked out, unable to hide the tears of mortification that had sprung to her eyes. She couldn't stand another minute of this utter humiliation. When she'd felt it once before, she'd vowed never to expose herself to it again, and so she wouldn't. This meeting was over.

While Mateo looked on, seeming distinctly nonplussed, she grabbed her coat and yanked it on, winding the scarf tightly around her neck, needing as many barriers between him and her as she could get.

'Rachel…' He stretched out one hand, his brows knitted together. He didn't understand. He thought she should be grateful for his attention, for the fact that he could kiss like a cross between

Prince Charming and Casanova. And that made Rachel even more furious, so her voice shook as she spoke her next words.

'You might think you're God's greatest gift to women, Mateo Karr—whatever, but that doesn't mean I'm about to fall into your lap like a plum ripe for the picking. As much as you so obviously thought I would.' She jabbed a finger into his powerful pecs for good measure, making his eyes widen.

'So you're handsome. So you're a good kisser. So you're an out-and-out prince. I don't care! I don't care a—a *fig* about any of it. I am *not* marrying you.' And with that final battle cry, the tears she'd tried to keep back spilling from her eyes, Rachel stalked out of the room.

CHAPTER SIX

WELL. THAT HADN'T gone exactly as he'd expected. In fact, it hadn't gone the way he'd expected at *all*—a failed experiment, if there ever was one.

Because if he'd truly been conducting an experiment, Mateo acknowledged with a grimace, he would have first made his aim.

To convince Rachel Lewis to marry him, and that physical compatibility would not be an issue for them.

And his prediction? That she would agree, and it wouldn't. And the variables? Well, how attracted they both would be, he supposed. And those had been *variable* indeed.

In fact, he didn't really like to think how variable their attraction had been. He'd been acting on instinct at first, sensing that Rachel needed proof that physicality between them would not be a problem. And from the moment his lips had brushed hers—no, from the moment he'd put his hands on her arms, felt her warm softness, and drawn her to him—he'd known there was no problem at all.

In fact, the *lack* of problem suggested a problem. Because Mateo hadn't expected that variable, hadn't expected to want more and more from the woman who had become so pliant in his arms.

Well, he told himself now, there had been another variable—the fact that he hadn't had sex in a very long time, and so his response had to have been predicated on that. Explainable. Simple. It didn't *mean* anything. It certainly didn't mean he had some sort of ridiculously overwhelming attraction to Rachel Lewis, when he hadn't looked at her that way even once in ten years.

Which right now felt like a comfort. He could be attracted to her, but it wasn't a force in his life. It wasn't something he would have to keep under control.

Not that it mattered anyway, because she'd stormed out of here as if she never intended seeing him again.

So what should his next step be? Why had she been so offended by his kiss? He'd felt her response, so he knew it wasn't some sort of maidenly revulsion. He thought of her words—*'You might think you're God's greatest gift to women...'*

He hardly thought that, of course. Admittedly, he'd never had trouble finding sexual partners, not that he'd had all that many. He was too focused on his work and too discerning in his companions to sleep around, but it certainly wasn't for lack of interest on women's—*many* women's—part. But Mateo didn't think he was arrogant about it, and he hadn't been proving to Rachel how attractive she found him, but rather how good they could be together.

And the answer was they could be quite surprisingly good indeed.

So why had she been annoyed? Why had she seemed, rather alarmingly, *hurt*?

Mateo was still musing on this when there was a tap on the door. Expecting the waiter back, to deliver the main course they now wouldn't be eating, he barked a command to enter.

The door creaked open slowly and Rachel appeared. Her hair was in damp tendrils around her face, and the shoulders of her coat were wet. The look she gave him was one of abashed humour.

'I think I may have been a little bit of a drama queen there,' she said, and Mateo nearly laughed with the relief of having her back, smiling at him.

'At least you were a queen,' he returned with a small smile. 'I knew you had it in you.'

She laughed ruefully and shook her head. 'This is all so crazy, Mateo.'

'I agree that it seems crazy, but how many experiments have we conducted over the years that others said were crazy? Or pointless? Or just wouldn't work?'

She bit her lip, white teeth sinking into pink lushness, making Mateo remember exactly how those lips had felt. Tasted. 'Quite a few.'

'And this is just another experiment. The ultimate experiment.' It sounded so clever and neat, but a shadow had entered Rachel's eyes.

'And what happens when the experiment fails?'

'It won't.' He answered swiftly, too swiftly. She wasn't convinced.

'We write up the lab results? Draw some conclusions? *Marriages between princes and commoners are not a good idea.*'

'I admit, the experiment analogy only goes so far. And you only have to look at this country's royal family to know that a marriage between a prince and a commoner has an excellent chance of success.'

'Or not.'

'The point is, our marriage can be successful. There's absolutely no reason for it not to be.'

'Isn't there?' There was a note of sorrowful vulnerability in her voice that made Mateo tense. And this had all been starting to look so promising.

'Are you referring to something specific?' he asked in as reasonable a tone as he could manage.

She sighed, shrugging off her wet coat as she

sat back down at the table. It seemed they would be eating their main course, after all. 'Yes and no, I suppose.'

Mateo took his own seat. 'As you know, there are no yes-and-no situations in science.'

'This isn't science. But it may be chemistry.' She met his gaze evenly, her expression determined.

'Physical chemistry,' Mateo stated, because it was obvious. 'You think we don't have it? I thought I proved—'

'You proved you were a good kisser,' Rachel cut across him. 'And that you can…make me respond to you.'

He frowned, wishing he could figure out what was bothering her, and why it was so much. 'And that is a problem?'

'It's not a problem. It's just…an inequality.' She looked away, blinking rapidly, and Mateo realised that no matter her seemingly calm and practical exterior, something about their kiss had affected her deeply, and not on a physical level.

'Why were you a drama queen, Rachel?' he asked slowly, feeling his way through the words. 'What made you respond so…emotionally?'

She was silent, her expression distant as she looked away from him, and Mateo decided not to press.

'When are our main courses coming?' she finally asked. 'I stormed out of here without eating my salad, and I'm starving.'

'So why did you storm out of here, exactly?' Mateo asked, taking the obvious opening. Rachel paused, her once determined gaze sliding away from his. Whatever it was, she clearly didn't want to tell him. 'Rachel,' he said gently, 'if we're going to be married, I need to know.'

She swung back towards him, her face drawn in lines of laughing disbelief. '"If we're going to be married"? A little cocksure, aren't you, Mateo?'

'I meant hypothetically,' he returned smoothly. 'If it's something you're thinking about even remotely…and you must be, because you came back here.'

'Maybe I came back here because I value your friendship.'

'That too.'

'And I didn't want to look like a prima donna.'

'Three reasons, then.'

She laughed and shook her head. 'Oh, Mateo. If we don't get married, I will miss you.'

Something leapt inside him and he leaned forward. 'Then marry me, Rachel.' His voice throbbed with more intent than he wanted to reveal. More desire.

Her eyes widened as her gaze moved over his face, as if she were trying to plumb the depths of him, and Mateo didn't want that. He held her gaze but he schooled his expression into something calm and determined. How he really felt.

'The reason I might have overreacted,' she said slowly, her gaze still on his face, 'is because I've… I've been burned before. By an arrogant man who thought I'd be grateful for his attentions, and then made a joke of them afterwards.'

Mateo didn't like the sound of that at *all*. Everything in him tightened as he answered levelly, 'Tell me more.'

She shrugged, spreading her hands. 'Sadly there's not much more to tell. He was a doctoral student when I was in my second year at Oxford—he paid me special attention, I thought he cared. He didn't, and he let people know it.' Her lips tightened as she looked away.

What was that supposed to mean? 'He hurt you?' Mateo asked, amazed at how much he disliked the thought. Not just disliked, but *detested*, with a deep, gut-churning emotion he didn't expect or want to feel.

'Emotionally, yes, he did. But I got over it.' Rachel lifted her chin, a gesture born of bravery. 'I didn't love him, not like that. But my ego was bruised, and I felt humiliated and hurt, and I decided for myself that I was never going to let another man treat me that way ever again, and so far I haven't.'

Realisation trickled icily through him and he jerked back a little. 'And you think I did? Was?'

'It felt like that at the time, but, I admit, I probably overreacted, due to my past experience.' She shrugged again. 'So now you know.'

Yet he didn't know, not really. He didn't know what this vile man had done, or how exactly he'd humiliated Rachel. He didn't know how she'd responded, or how long it had taken her to recover and heal. But Mateo was reluctant to ask any more, to know any more. It was her private pain, and she'd tell him if she wanted to. Besides, information was responsibility, and he had enough of that to be going on with.

'I'm sorry,' he said. 'For what happened. And how I made you feel.'

'You didn't mean to. At least I don't think you did. Which is why I'm still here.' She gave him one of her old grins. 'That, and the risotto that had better be here soon.'

'I assure you, it is.' Mateo reached for his phone and texted the maître d' of the restaurant, whom he'd contacted earlier to make the reservation. Within seconds the waiter was back, with two more silver-domed dishes.

'So if you really are a prince,' Rachel asked after he'd whisked the lids off and left, 'where's your security detail? Why isn't there a guy in a dark suit with a walkie-talkie in the corner of the room?'

'That would be a rather unpleasant breach of privacy,' Mateo returned. 'He's outside in the hall.'

Rachel nearly dropped her fork. '*Is* he?'

'Of course.'

She shook her head slowly. 'Did you have security all the time in Cambridge? Was I just completely blind?'

'No, I didn't. I chose not to. As the third in line to the throne, I had that freedom.'

'But you don't any more.'

His lips and gut both tightened. 'No.'

Rachel watched Mateo's expression shutter with a flicker of curiosity, and a deeper ripple of compassion. 'Do you want to be king?' she asked and he stiffened, the shutter coming down even more.

'It's not a question of want. It's my duty.'

'You didn't actually answer me.'

His mouth thinned as he inclined his head. 'Very well. I want to do my duty.'

Which sounded rather grim. Rachel took a forkful of risotto and chewed slowly. It was delicious, rich and creamy, but she barely registered the flavour as her mind whirled. Was she really thinking seriously about saying yes to Mateo's shocking proposal?

It had struck her, as she'd stormed away from the restaurant and got soaked in the process, that she was a little too outraged. It was easier to feel outraged, to wrap herself in it like a cloak of armour, than to think seriously about what Mateo was suggesting.

And yet the farther she'd walked, the more she'd realised she had to be sensible about this. She had to be the scientist she'd always been. She couldn't sail on the high tide of emotion, not for long. It simply wasn't in her nature.

And so she'd gone back, and now she was here, thinking seriously about saying yes.

'So what would a marriage between us look like?' she asked. 'On a day-to-day basis?'

'We'd live in the royal palace in Constanza,' Mateo answered with calm swiftness. 'It is a beautiful place, built five hundred years ago, right on the sea.'

'Okay…'

'As I said before, you could choose your involvement in various charities and initiatives. Admittedly, there would be a fair amount of ribbon cutting and clapping, that sort of thing. It's unavoidable, I'm afraid.'

'I don't mind that. But I don't exactly look the part, do I?' She had to say it.

Mateo looked distinctly nonplussed. 'So you've intimated before. If you mean clothes, I assure you, you will be provided with a complete wardrobe of your choice, along with personal stylists and hairdressers as you wish.'

'So like Cinderella.' She didn't know how she felt about that. A little excited? A little insulted? A little afraid? All three, and more than a little.

Mateo shrugged. 'Like any royal princess—or queen.'

'And what about children?' Rachel asked. Her stomach quivered at the thought. 'You mentioned needing an heir as soon as possible.'

'Yes.'

'That's kind of a big thing, Mateo.'

'I agree.'

'You don't even know if I want children.'

'I assume we would not be having this discussion if you were completely averse to the idea.'

Rachel sighed and laid down her fork. Her stomach was churning too much to eat. 'I don't even know,' she admitted. 'I haven't let myself think about it.'

Mateo frowned, his gaze searching her face. 'Let yourself?'

'I'm thirty-two, and I haven't had a serious relationship since university. I assumed it wasn't likely to happen.'

'Well, now you can assume differently.'

'Assuming I can get pregnant in the first place.'

He shrugged. 'Is there any reason you believe you cannot?'

'No.' She couldn't believe they were talking about having a baby together so clinically, and yet somehow it didn't surprise her at all. Mateo was approaching the whole matter of their marriage in as scientific a way as possible, which she didn't mind, not exactly.

'What about love?' she asked baldly. 'I know you didn't approach me because of love, but is it something that could happen in time? Something you'd hope for?' A long silence ensued, which told her everything.

'Is that something you would wish?' Mateo asked finally. 'Something you would hope for?'

Which sounded pathetic, and was the exact reason why she'd thought this whole idea was ridiculous in the first place. Well, that and a lot of other reasons, too.

And yet…was it? Did she want the fairy-tale romance, to fall head over heels in love with someone? With *Mateo*? Falling head over heels sounded painful. And from her limited experience with Josh, it had been. Did she really want that again, just because everyone around her—on TV, in books—seemed to assume it was?

When she and Mateo had first started working together, she'd had a bit of a crush on him and she'd worked to get over it. And she *had*. Did she really want to feel that soul-pinching, gut-churning sensation of liking someone more than he liked you, and in this case to a much more serious degree? Wouldn't it be easier if they just both agreed to keep that off the table for ever?

'Honestly, I don't know,' she said slowly. 'It's what everyone assumes you should want.'

'Maybe between the pages of a book like the one on your coffee table, but not in real life. Feelings like that fade, Rachel. What we have—what we could have—would be real.'

'You don't need to sound quite so dismissive about the whole idea,' Rachel returned.

'Not dismissive,' Mateo countered. 'Sensible. And I think you're sensible, as well.' He held her gaze, his aquamarine eyes like lasers. Not for the first time, Rachel wondered why he had to be so beautiful. It would be so much easier if he was more normal looking. Average.

'So you're not interested in falling in love?' she asked, unsure if her tone was pathetic or joking or somewhere in between. 'I just want to make sure.'

Mateo was silent for a long, painful moment. 'No,' he said finally. 'I am not.'

She nodded, absorbing that, recognising that at least then the whole issue would be off the table. Not something to be discussed or hoped for, ever. Could she live with that? Was she *sensible* enough? 'I have my mother to consider,' she said at last, hardly able to believe they were now talking about real practicalities. 'She has Alzheimer's. She needs my care.'

'That is not a problem. She can accompany us to Kallyria, where she will receive top medical care, her own suite of rooms, and a full-time nurse.'

'I don't know if she could cope with that much change. She struggled to move here from Sussex.'

'If it is preferable, she could stay in Cambridge. I can arrange her care at the best residential facility in the area immediately.'

Rachel sighed. Thinking of her mother made her feel anxious—and guilty. Because the thought of escaping the mundanity of her life with her mother, the constant complaining and criticism that she'd faced her whole life and that had become only worse with her mother's disease, was wonderfully liberating.

'I don't know,' she said at last. 'I suppose I could discuss it with her.' A prospect that made her stomach cramp.

'If it helps, I could do that with you,' Mateo said, and for a second Rachel felt as if she'd put on a pair of 3D glasses. She could see the whole world in an entirely different dimension.

If she married Mateo, she wouldn't have to do everything alone. She'd have someone advocating for her, supporting her, and backing her up.

Someone to laugh with, to share life with, to discuss ideas and sleep next to. What did love have on any of that? Suddenly, blindingly, it was obvious. Wonderfully obvious.

'Thank you,' she said after a moment, her voice shaky, her mind still spinning.

'It's not a problem at all.' Mateo paused, his hands flat on the table as he gave her a direct look. 'While I recognise the seriousness of your decision, and the understandable need for time to consider, I am afraid matters are quite pressing. The situation in my country is urgent.'

'Urgent?'

'The instability of rule has led to a rise in insurgency. Nothing that cannot be dealt with, but it means I need to be back in Kallyria, firmly on my throne, my wife at my side, as soon as possible.'

'How soon as possible do you mean?' Rachel asked as she grappled with the whole idea of insurgency and Mateo needing to deal with it.

'Tomorrow would be best.'

'Tomorrow...?' She gaped at him. 'Mateo, I'd have to give at least a term's notice—'

'That can be dealt with.'

'My mother—'

'Again, it can be dealt with.'

'My flat...'

'I can arrange for it to be sold or kept, as you wish.'

She'd worked hard to save for that flat. Prices in Cambridge had skyrocketed over the last decade and, even on a researcher's salary, buying the flat had been a stretch. Rachel took a quick, steadying breath. 'I don't know. This is a lot quicker than I expected.'

'I understand.' Yet his tone was implacable. He understood, but he would not change the terms. And that, Rachel realised, was an attitude she would encounter and have to accept again and again if she said yes.

'I don't know,' she said at last. 'Can I think about it for a little while, at least? A night, and I'll tell you first thing in the morning?'

Mateo hesitated, and Rachel knew even that felt like too long to him. Then he gave a brief nod. 'Very well. But if you do say yes, Rachel, I will have to put things in motion very quickly.'

'I understand.'

He hesitated, then reached over and covered her hand with his own, his palm warm and large and comforting on hers. 'I know this all seems quite overwhelming. There are so many different things to consider. But I do believe, Rachel, I believe completely, that we could have a very successful and happy marriage. I wouldn't be here if I didn't believe that absolutely.'

She nodded, pressing her lips together to keep them from trembling. Already she knew what her answer would be.

CHAPTER SEVEN

RACHEL PEERED OUT of the window as the misty grey fog of an English autumn grew smaller below and the plane lifted into a bright azure sky. It was the day after Mateo's proposal, and they were on the royal Kallyrian jet, for an overnight flight to Constanza.

Rachel's head was still spinning from how quickly everything had happened. Mateo had escorted her home, kissed her cheek, and told her he would ring her at seven in the morning for her answer.

Back in her flat, with her mother parked in front of a television on highest volume and the burnt smell of her toastie still hanging in the air, Rachel had felt the smallness of her existence descend on her like a thick fog. When she'd opened a patronising email from Supercilious Simon, it had been the push she hadn't even needed.

She was going to say yes. As crazy as it seemed, as risky as it might be, she believed in her heart that life was meant for living, not just existing, and without Mateo in it that was what hers had become. A matter of survival.

She spent a sleepless night trying to imagine her future and unable to come up with anything more than hazy, vague scenes out of a Grace Kelly film, or maybe *The Princess Diaries*. When her mobile buzzed next to her bed at seven o'clock precisely, her stomach whirled with nerves—but also excitement.

'Mateo?'

'Have you decided?'

She took a breath, let it fill her lungs. She felt as if she were leaping and twirling into outer space. 'Yes,' she said softly. 'I say yes.'

Mateo had sprung instantly into action. He'd disconnected the call almost immediately, saying he would come over within the next half-hour to begin arrangements.

'My mother…' Rachel had begun, starting to panic. 'She doesn't do well with change…'

'We will make her transition as smooth as possible,' Mateo promised her, and it had been. He'd left her mother speechless and simpering under the full wattage of his charm, and that very afternoon the three of them had toured the high-end nursing home on the outskirts of Cambridge that had a private facility for memory-impaired residents.

Carol had seemed remarkably pleased with it all—the private room was far larger and more luxurious than the one she currently had, and the nursing home had a full schedule of activities. And when Rachel had explained she would be moving away, her mother hadn't been bothered in the least. Not, Rachel acknowledged with a sigh, that that had been much of a surprise.

Still, it all seemed so incredibly, head-spinningly fast. Her mother was already settled in the nursing home; Rachel and Mateo had moved her over that very evening. A lump had formed in Rachel's throat as she'd hugged her mother goodbye. Who knew when or if she'd see her again? Yet her mother had barely seemed aware of her departure; she'd turned away quickly, intent on investigating the lounge area with its large flat-screen TV. As she'd watched her mother shuffle away, it had seemed hard to believe that she'd once been the sophisticated and erudite wife of a prominent academic.

'Bye, Mum,' she'd whispered, and then she'd walked away without looking back.

Back at her flat, Rachel had packed her things up in a single suitcase, since Mateo had assured her she would not need anything once she was in Kallyria; all would be provided. He advised only to take keepsakes and mementoes, of which she had very few.

It felt a little sad, a bit pathetic, to leave an entire life behind so easily. She'd email her friends once she reached Kallyria, and Mateo had promised her that he would pay for anyone she wished to attend the wedding to be flown over. He'd dealt with her job situation, and she'd felt a flicker of sorrow that, after ten years, she could both walk away and be let go so easily. But Cambridge was a transient place; people moved in and out all the time. Even after ten years, she was just one more.

Still, Rachel told herself as the royal jet levelled out, there was no point in being melancholy. She was about to embark on the adventure of a lifetime, and she wanted to enjoy it.

She glanced at Matteo, who was sitting across from her in a sumptuous seat of white leather, frowning down at his laptop. Since securing her hand in marriage, he had paid very little attention to her, but Rachel hadn't minded. He had much to attend to, a country to rule and, besides, she wasn't one to want to be fussed over.

Still, she wouldn't have minded a bit of conversation now.

'I feel like we should have champagne,' she said a bit playfully, and Mateo looked up from his screen with a frown.

'Champagne? Of course.' He snapped his fingers and a steward materialised silently, as if plucked from the air.

'Yes, Your Highness?'

That was something that was going to take a lot of getting used to. Despite Mateo's obvious and understated displays of both wealth and power, she realised she hadn't fully believed in the whole king thing until she'd stepped on the royal jet, and everyone had started bowing and curtseying and 'Your Highnessing' him. It had been weird.

The steward produced a bottle of bubbly with the kind of label Rachel could only dream of, popped the cork and poured two crystalline flutes full.

'Cheers,' Rachel said a bit tartly. During this whole elegant procedure, Mateo hadn't so much as looked up from his screen.

She took a large sip of the champagne, which was crisp and delicious on her tongue. Another sip, and finally Mateo looked up.

He took in the open bottle chilling in a silver bucket, his untouched flute, and Rachel's expression with a small, rueful smile.

'I apologise.' He reached for his glass and touched it to hers, his gaze warm and intent. 'As we say in Kallyria, *yamas*.'

'I don't even know what language that is,' Rachel confessed, wrinkling her nose. 'Or what language you speak in Kallyria.'

'It is Greek, and it means health or, more prosaically, cheers.'

'Do you speak Greek?'

'Yes, and Turkish.'

'Wow.' She realised how little she knew about, well, *anything*. 'I should have done an Internet search on you last night.'

He arched an eyebrow. 'You didn't?'

'I was too busy thinking about whether or not I was going to marry you.' Although really she'd already decided. She'd spent most of the evening walking around in a daze, doing nothing productive.

'You can ask me what you like. There will be a lot to learn.'

'Yes.' Rachel could see that already. 'What's going to happen when we land?'

'I've had our arrival at Constanza embargoed—'

'What does that mean?'

'I am not alerting the media and no press will be allowed.'

'Okay.' She tried to process that for a moment, and failed. 'Why?'

'Because I want to control all the information,' Mateo answered swiftly. 'When we arrive at the royal palace, I will take you to meet my mother.'

Rachel swallowed. 'Have you told her about me?'

'Yes, she is greatly looking forward to making your acquaintance.'

'That's nice,' Rachel said faintly. She didn't know why she was starting to feel so alarmed; she'd known this was the kind of thing she was signing up for. And yet now it was starting to feel so very *real*. 'And then what?'

'Then you will meet with your stylist and hairdresser,' Mateo answered. 'They are temporary only, as I am sure you will like to select your own staff when the times comes.'

'I've never had staff before,' Rachel said with a nervous laugh. She took a gulp of champagne to steady her nerves.

'You do now.' Mateo nodded towards the stewards in the front cabin of the aircraft. 'Everyone who works for me works for you.'

'Right.' Something else she could not get her head around.

'When you have finished with the stylists, you will be introduced to Kallyria.'

'Introduced to a country? How is that meant to happen?' Already her mouth was drying, her heart beginning to hammer at the thought.

'There is a balcony from where royalty has traditionally made all such announcements. I shall introduce you, we will wave, and then retire into the palace. Some time in the next week we will hold an engagement ball where you will meet all the dignitaries and statesmen you need to, and then we will marry next Saturday.'

'Wait, what? That's only a week from now.'

Mateo's brows snapped together as he regarded her evenly, his flute of champagne held between two long, lean fingers. 'Is that a problem? You are aware of the urgency of the situation.'

Rachel swallowed dryly. 'It's not a problem. Just…give me a moment to get my head around it.'

'Very well.' Mateo turned back to his laptop, and Rachel sipped the last of her champagne, her mind feeling like so much buzzing noise. After a few moments she excused herself with a murmur and went to the back of the plane, where there was a sumptuous bedroom with a king-sized bed and an en suite bathroom all in marble.

Rachel sank onto the bed and looked around her in as much of a daze as ever, if not more. What was she doing here, really?

Mateo straightened the cuffs of his suit as he waited for Rachel to emerge from the bedroom where she was changing into a fresh outfit to exit the plane.

He'd spent the majority of the flight working, grabbing an hour of sleep in his seat while Rachel had retired to the bedroom as soon as she'd drunk her champagne, and she hadn't come out again until an hour before landing.

Mateo had checked in on her halfway through

the flight, and seen her still in her clothes, curled up on top of the covers, fast asleep. Her hair was spread across the pillow just as he'd once imagined, and as he gazed at her he realised he'd never seen her sleep before, and yet from now on he would many times over.

The thought had brought a shaft of—something—to him. Something he wasn't sure he wanted to name, because he couldn't discern how it made him feel.

He'd rushed into marriage because he'd had to, and he'd done it with Rachel because at least he knew and trusted her. But watching her sleep, he was accosted by the realisation of how intimate their lives together would have to be, no matter how much he kept a certain part of himself closed off, a part that he hadn't accessed in fifteen years, since Cressida.

No matter how physically intimate they might be, no matter how close they might become, Mateo knew there was only so much he could ever offer Rachel. Only so much he knew how to give, and he had to trust that it would be enough. It certainly would be for him, and it had better be for her, because he didn't have anything else.

Straightening his tie, he gave his reflection one last glance before he went to knock on the bedroom door.

'We're landing in twenty minutes, Rachel. We need to take our seats.'

'All right.' She opened the door, throwing her shoulders back as she gave him a smile that bordered on terrified. 'Do I look all right?'

'You look fine,' Mateo assured her, because the media wouldn't be there and so it didn't matter. In truth he acknowledged that she would benefit from the help of a stylist. The shapeless trouser suit and plain ponytail that had served her so well for over ten years in academia were not exactly the right look for a queen, something he suspected Rachel was completely aware of. She certainly seemed aware of any potential deficiencies in her persona, and Mateo was determined to assuage her concerns.

'Did you sleep well?' he asked as he took her elbow and escorted her to the front of the plane. She gave him a strange look, and he realised it wasn't something he would have normally done... *touch* her. Yet he acknowledged he needed to start acting like a husband, not a colleague, and in any case he found he wanted to do it, his fingers light on her elbow, her breast brushing his arm as they walked. Was she aware of it? She didn't seem to be, but he most certainly was.

'Better than I expected,' Rachel answered with a little laugh. 'I think I was so exhausted because I didn't sleep a wink the night before!'

'Didn't you?'

She gave him a wry, laughing look. 'No, I most certainly did not. I stayed up the entire night wondering if I was going to marry you, and trying to imagine what that would look like, because frankly I still find it impossible.'

'Yet very soon you will find out.'

'I know.' She fiddled with the seat buckle, her gaze lowered so her ponytail fell forward onto her shoulder, like a curling ribbon of chocolate-brown silk. For some reason he couldn't quite understand, Mateo reached forward and flicked it back. Rachel glanced at him, startled. He smiled blandly.

'Tell me about your mother,' she blurted.

'My mother? Her name is Agathe and she is a very strong and gracious woman. I admire her very much.'

'She sounds completely intimidating.'

Mateo frowned. 'She isn't.'

'I don't believe you. You're intimidating.' Rachel gave him a teasing smile, but Mateo knew she was serious—and scared. He could see it in her eyes, in the way she blinked rapidly, her lush lashes fanning downwards again and again as she moistened her lips with the tip of a delectably pink tongue.

'You've known me for ten years, Rachel,' he

pointed out reasonably. 'How can I be intimidating?'

'You're different now,' she answered with a shrug. 'Until yesterday, I never saw you snap your fingers at someone before.'

Mateo acknowledged the point with a rueful nod. 'I don't think I had, at least not while at Cambridge.'

'You seem so used to all this luxury and wealth. I mean, I suppose you grew up with it, and I knew you had a fancy house in Cambridge because of some investments or something…'

He raised his eyebrows. 'Is that courtesy of the university gossips?'

Rachel smiled, unabashed. 'Yes.'

'Well, it wasn't investments. It was a company I founded. Lyric Tech.'

'What, you just *founded* a company in your spare time?'

He shrugged. 'I had an idea for a music app and it went from there.'

'As it does.' Rachel pursed her lips, looking troubled. 'See, when you say stuff like that, I feel as if I really don't know you at all.'

'You know me, Rachel.' He hadn't meant his voice to sound so low and meaningful, or to caress the syllables of her name quite so much, but they did. Her eyes widened and a faint blush touched her cheeks as she stared at him for a second before looking away.

'Maybe we should talk about molecular electrocatalysis or something?' she suggested shakily. 'Just to feel like our old selves again.'

'If you like.' Mateo relaxed back into his seat. He was always happy to talk shop. 'What are your thoughts on the metal-to-metal hydrogen atom transfer?'

Rachel looked surprised that he was playing along, but then a little smile curved her mouth and she considered the question properly. 'I suppose you're talking about iron and chromium?'

'Indeed.'

'There are some limitations, of course.' They spent the next fifteen minutes discussing the potential benefits of the new research on various forms of renewable energy, and she became so engrossed in the discussion that Rachel didn't even notice the plane landing, or taxiing along the private airstrip. It was only when she glanced out of the window and saw several blacked-out sedans with a small army of people in front of them that her face paled and she gulped audibly.

'Mateo, I don't know if I can do this.'

'Of course you can,' he answered calmly. He meant it; he'd seen her handle a dozen more demanding situations back at Cambridge. All she had to do now was walk out of the plane and into a waiting car. 'You are going to be my queen, Rachel. The only one who doubts whether you are up for the role is you.'

She gave him a wry look. 'Are you sure about that?'

'Positive.' If anyone else doubted it, he would make sure they stopped immediately. He would not allow for anyone to doubt or deride his chosen queen.

Rachel glanced back out at the sedans, and the flank of waiting security, all looking suitably blank-faced, and Mateo watched with pride as the iron entered her soul. She nodded slowly as she straightened her shoulders, her chin tilting upward as her eyes blazed briefly with gold.

'All right,' she said. 'Let's do this.'

Moments later the security team were opening the door to the plane, and Mateo reached for Rachel's hand. Hers was icy-cold and he twined his fingers through hers and gently drew her closer to his side. Her smile trembled on her lips as she shot him a questioning look. This closeness was new to both of them, but Mateo didn't mind it.

'Ready?' he asked softly, and, setting her jaw, she nodded.

Then together they stepped out of the plane, onto the stairs. They walked side by side down the rather rickety stairs to the waiting car, and Mateo nodded at the security team, who all bowed in response, their faces remaining impressively impassive. Mateo did not explain who Rachel was; they would find out soon enough. They could almost certainly guess.

Pride blossomed in his soul as she kept her chin tilted and her back ramrod straight as she walked from the bottom of the stairs to the waiting car. She was, Mateo acknowledged with a deep tremor of satisfaction, fit to be his queen.

CHAPTER EIGHT

THE WORLD BLURRED by as Rachel sat in the sedan and it sped along wide boulevards, the sea glittering blue on the other side of the road, palm trees proudly pointing to an azure sky.

Since exiting the plane, Rachel had felt as if she were disembodied, watching everything unfold as if from far above. She couldn't possibly be sitting in a luxury sedan with blacked-out windows, an armed guard travelling before and behind and a man set to be king brooding next to her, on her way to an actual palace?

It had been utterly surreal to walk down those steps and see the guards bowing to Mateo—and her. She'd seen their impassive faces and recognised the look of people well trained to keep their expressions to themselves. Had they guessed she was Mateo's bride, their next queen? Or did they assume she was some dowdy secretary brought along to take dictation? That was what she would have assumed, if she'd been in their place.

As much as she was trying to keep from getting down on herself, Rachel had to acknowledge the struggle was real. Her trouser suit was five years old and bought on the bargain rack, because she'd never cared about clothes. She had no make-up on because when she tried to use it, she looked like a clown. Her hair hadn't been cut in six months at least. Yes, she was definitely feeling like the dowdy secretary rather than the defiant queen.

'If I'd known I was going to become a queen this week,' she quipped to Mateo, 'I would have had my hair cut and lost a stone.'

He turned to her, his expression strangely fierce, his face drawn into stark lines of determination. 'Neither is necessary, I assure you.'

She eyed him sceptically. 'Didn't you mention a team of stylists and beauticians waiting at the palace to turn me into some kind of post-godmother Cinderella?'

'It doesn't mean you need to change.'

Rachel glanced down at her trouser suit. 'I think I might,' she said. 'At least this outfit.' She didn't want to dwell on all the other ways she might need to change, and so she chose to change the subject. 'So what is the royal palace like? Besides being palatial, naturally.'

A small smile twitched the corner of Mateo's mouth. 'And royal.'

'Obvs.'

'It's five hundred years old, built on the sea, looking east. It has magnificent gardens leading down to the beach, and many beautiful terraces and balconies. You will occupy the Queen's suite of rooms after our marriage.'

'You need to stop saying stuff like that, because I feel like I'm living in a fairy tale.'

His smile deepened as he glanced down at her, aquamarine eyes sparkling. 'But it's true.'

'And where will I be before our marriage?' Which was now in six *days*, something she couldn't let herself think about without panicking.

'A guest suite. But first, remember, my mother wishes to meet you.'

'Right away?' Rachel swallowed hard. 'Before anything else?'

'It is important.'

And terrifying. Rachel tried to moderate her breathing as the car sped on, past whitewashed buildings with terracotta roofs, flowers blooming everywhere, spilling out of pots and window boxes. She gazed at a woman with a basket of oranges on her head, and a man with a white turban riding a rusty bicycle. Kallyria was a place where the east and west met, full of history and colour and life. And it was now her home.

The reality of it all, the enormity of the choice

she had made, slammed into her again and again, leaving her breathless.

After about ten minutes, the motorcade drove through high, ornate gates of wrought iron, and then down a sweeping drive, a palace of sparkling white stone visible in the distance. It was a combination of fairy-tale castle and luxury Greek villa—complete with terraces and turrets, latticed shutters and trailing bougainvillea at every window, and Rachel thought there had to be at least a hundred.

'Welcome home,' Mateo said with a smile, and she nearly choked. She felt as if she were caught up in a riptide of officialdom as she was ushered out of the car and into the soaring marble foyer of the palace, a twisting, double staircase leading to a balcony above, and then onwards. A cupola high above them let in dazzling sunlight, and at least a dozen staff, the royal insignia on their uniform, were lined up waiting to bow or curtsey to Mateo.

'My mother is waiting upstairs, in her private parlour,' Mateo murmured, and, taking her by the elbow, he led her upstairs.

'Mitera?' he called, knocking on the wood-panelled door once, and when a mellifluous voice bid them to enter, he did.

Rachel followed, her knees practically knocking together. What if Mateo's mother didn't like her? What if she looked at her and wondered why on earth he'd chosen her as his bride? His queen?

The woman rising from a loveseat at one end of the elegant and spacious room was exactly what Rachel had expected, even though she had never seen a photograph of Agathe Karavitis.

She was tall and elegant, her dark blonde hair barely streaked with silver drawn back in a loose chignon. She wore a chic silk blouse tucked into wide-leg trousers and as she came forward, a welcoming smile on her face, her arms outstretched, she moved with an unconscious grace. Rachel felt like the dowdiest of dowds in comparison, and she tried not to let it show in her face as Agathe kissed both her cheeks and pressed her hands between her own.

'Rachel. I am so very delighted to make your acquaintance.'

'As I am yours,' Rachel managed to stammer. She felt woefully and wholly inadequate.

'I must check on a few things before we appear publicly,' Mateo informed her. Rachel tried not to gape at him in panic. He was leaving?

'She is in safe hands, I assure you,' Agathe said.

'We will appear on the balcony at two…' Mateo gave his mother a significant look.

'She will be ready.' She waved at him with an elegant hand. 'Go.'

Mateo gave Rachel a quick smile that did not reassure her at all and then strode out of the room.

'I have called for tea,' Agathe said once he had left, the door clicking firmly shut behind him. 'You must be exhausted.'

'I'm a bit tired, yes,' Rachel said carefully. She realised she had no idea how to handle this meeting. Despite Agathe's air of gracious friendliness, she had no idea how the woman really thought of her. According to Mateo, Agathe had drawn up a list of suitable brides, and Rachel had most certainly not been on it.

'Come sit down,' Agathe invited, patting the seat next to her. 'We have little time today to get to know one another, but tomorrow I have arranged for us to have breakfast together.'

'That's very kind.' Rachel perched on the edge of the loveseat while Agathe eyed her far too appraisingly. Rachel knew how she looked—how limp her ponytail, how creased her suit, how pasty her skin. She tried to smile.

'I suppose you are surprised,' she said finally, because as always she preferred confronting the truth rather than hiding from it. 'I am not the expected choice for your son's bride.'

'You are not,' Agathe agreed with a nod. 'And yet I think you might be exactly right.'

That surprised Rachel, and for the first time

in what felt like for ever she actually started to relax. 'You do?'

'Don't sound so surprised,' Agathe returned with a tinkling laugh. 'Did you think I would not approve?'

'I wondered.'

'More than anything, I wish my son to be happy,' Agathe said quietly. 'And the fact that he chose you, that he knows you and calls you his friend...that is important. Far more important than having the right pedigree or something similar.' She shrugged slim shoulders. 'It is a modern world. We are no longer in the days of princes and kings needing to marry young women of suitable social standing, thank goodness.'

Rachel wasn't sure how to reply. Her father had been a well-regarded academic, if a commoner, but she doubted that held much water in the world of royalty. 'Thank you for your understanding,' she said at last.

An attendant came in with a tea tray, and Agathe served, her movements as elegant as ever. 'I am afraid we have only a few moments, if we wish you to be ready for the announcement.'

Rachel's stomach cramped as she took a soothing sip of the tea. Swallowing, she said, 'I don't think I'll ever be ready.'

'Nonsense,' Agathe said briskly. 'You just need the right tools.'

* * *

Mateo felt the weight of responsibility drop heavily onto his shoulders as he took a seat at his father's desk. His desk now. How long would it take him to think of it like that? To think of himself as King?

Two days away had taken their toll, and now his narrowed gaze scanned the various reports that had come in during his absence. Increased unrest in the north of the country; the important economic talks on a knife edge; domestic policy careening towards a crisis. An emergency on every front, and in just three hours he and Rachel would step in front of the waiting crowds and he would announce his choice of bride.

At least he did not regret taking that decision. Although she clearly had doubts about her suitability, Mateo did not. His only concern was making sure their relationship did not veer into the overly emotional or intimate. As long as they stayed friends, they would be fine. He would make sure of it.

Mateo spent an hour going over reports before he decided to check on Rachel's progress with the stylists he'd engaged. After a member of staff informed him of their whereabouts, he strode towards the east wing of the palace, where the guest suites were housed. From behind the first door on the corridor he heard the accented trill of the woman who dressed his mother.

'Of course we will have to do something about those eyebrows...' Mateo stopped outside the door, frowning. 'And that *chin*...' The despair, bordering on disgust, in the woman's voice tightened his gut. 'Fortunately some—how do they say in the English?—contouring will help. As for the clothes...something flowing, to hide the worst.'

The worst?

Furious now, as well as incredulous, Mateo flung open the door. Four women, matchstick-thin and officious, buzzed around Rachel, who sat in a chair in front of a mirror, looking horribly resigned. At his entrance the women turned to him, wide-eyed, mouths open.

'What is going on here?' Mateo demanded, his voice a low growl of barely suppressed outrage.

The women all swept panicked curtsies that Mateo ignored.

'Your Highness...'

'What is going on?'

'We were just attending to Kyria Lewis...'

'In a manner I find most displeasing. You are all dismissed at once.' A shocked intake of breath was the only response he got, followed by a frozen silence.

'Mateo,' Rachel said softly. He turned his gaze

to her, saw her giving him one of her wonderfully wry smiles. 'Remember when I was being a drama queen? Don't be a drama king. They're just doing their job.'

'They insulted you,' he objected, his voice pulsating with fury. 'I will not have it.'

'They were just being pragmatic, and in any case they weren't saying anything I haven't said myself a thousand times before. I really don't like my chin.'

'Your chin is fine.'

Rachel's mouth quirked. 'Shall we argue about it?'

'Their comments and attitude are *not* acceptable.' He would not back down, no matter what damage mitigation Rachel felt she needed to do.

'Your Highness,' Francesca, the main stylist, said in a hesitant voice. 'Please accept my deepest apologies for my remarks. I was thinking out loud…but you are right, it was unacceptable.' She bowed her head. 'If you will give me this opportunity to style Kyria Lewis, I will do my utmost to help her succeed.'

'She will succeed with or without you,' Mateo snapped. 'You are not here to make her succeed, but simply to provide her with the right clothes and make-up.'

Francesca's head dipped lower. 'As you say,' she murmured.

'Mateo.' Rachel's voice was gentle. 'Honestly, it's okay.'

But it wasn't. He saw so clearly how she accepted being belittled, how she thought because she was curvy and dressed in shapeless clothes she wasn't worth the same as a woman with a wasp-like waist and a similar attitude. Mateo hated it.

'You will dress and style Kyria Lewis,' he instructed the women, his eyes like lasers on the penitent Francesca. 'I will review the terms of your contract with the palace myself before the day is out.'

The women murmured their thanks and he strode out of the room, still battling an inexplicable fury. Why did he care so much? Rachel didn't. Why couldn't he just let it go? Yet he found he couldn't.

He'd never considered Rachel's feelings in such a specific way before he'd decided to marry her. He'd never considered *anyone's* feelings, he acknowledged with wry grimness, not really.

Not since Cressida, whose feelings he had considered both far too much and not nearly enough. The paradox of his relationship with her, the manic highs and terrible lows, was something he knew he wasn't strong enough to experience again. And even though Rachel was entirely different, he feared the root cause of those emotions was the same. *Love.* Best to avoid.

And yet now, despite his determination to keep a certain aloofness, and for reasons he did not wish to probe too deeply, he felt as if he was changing. Now he cared—admittedly about something relatively small, but still. It mattered. It mattered to him.

Wanting to leave such disturbing thoughts behind, Mateo went to meet with the palace press officer and arrange the last details of their appearance on the main balcony. All the country's press would be assembled in the courtyard below, along with most of Europe's and some of Asia's.

Kallyria was a small country, but since the discovery of oil beneath its lands, it had become a major player on the world stage. The whole world would be waiting for and watching this announcement. Mateo wanted to make sure everything was ready—and perfect.

At quarter to two, the door to the reception room whose French windows opened onto the main balcony opened, and Francesca ushered Rachel in, beaming with pride.

Mateo gave her a level look, still unimpressed by her behaviour, before turning his attention to his soon-to-be wife…and then trying not to let his jaw drop.

Rachel looked…like Rachel, yet more. Her hair

had been trimmed and was styled in loose waves about her face, soft and glossy. She wore minimal make-up, but it highlighted everything Mateo liked about her—her lush and rosy lips, her dark eyes with their luxuriant lashes, and cheekbones that he hadn't actually noticed before but now couldn't tear his gaze away from.

She wore a simple wrap dress in forest-green silk—a dress that clung without being too revealing and made the most of the generous curves Mateo longed to touch and explore. Her shapely calves were encased in sheer tights, and accentuated by a pair of elegant black heels.

'Well?' Her voice held a questioning lilt that bordered on uncertainty. 'Will I pass?'

'You will more than pass.' Mateo gave Francesca a grudging nod. 'I meant what I said earlier, but I will admit you have done well.'

'Thank you, Your Highness.' She bobbed a curtsey and then was gone. Rachel walked slowly towards him, grimacing a little.

'I'm tottering. I know it. I'm not used to heels.'

'All you'll have to do is step through those doors and stand still.'

She shot a worried look towards the gauze-covered windows. 'How many people are out there?'

Mateo knew there was no point in dissembling. 'Quite a few.'

Rachel nodded and ran her hands down the

sides of her dress. 'Okay.' She threw back her shoulders and lifted her chin, as she'd done before when she was gathering her courage. He loved to see it.

'I don't look ridiculous, do I?' she asked in a low voice. 'You know, silk purse, sow's ear…'

'Rachel.' Mateo stared at her incredulously. 'You look amazing. Gorgeous, vibrant, full of life, *sexy.*' The words spilled from him with conviction; they *had* to be said.

She stared at him for a moment, her lips parting, her eyes widening. Belatedly Mateo realised how intent he'd sounded, how involved. He cleared his throat, but before he could say anything more the press officer stepped forward.

'If we could go over the schedule, Your Highness?'

'Yes, in a moment.' He waved the man aside before drawing the small black velvet box out of his jacket pocket. 'You need one more thing to complete your outfit.' Her eyes had widened at the sight of the box, and she didn't speak. Mateo opened it to reveal a blue diamond encircled with smaller white diamonds, set on a ring of white gold. 'This is the Kallyrian Blue. It has been in the royal family for six hundred years.'

'Oh, my goodness…' She looked up at him with genuine panic. 'Can I please wear a fake? I cannot be responsible for a jewel that size.'

'It is heavily insured, don't worry. And it belongs to you now. It has always been the Queen's engagement ring.'

'Your mother…'

'Was more than happy to pass it on.'

Rachel let out a shaky breath. 'Whoo, boy.' She held out her hand, and Mateo slipped the ring onto her finger.

'There. Perfect.'

'It's so heavy.' She let out a breathy, incredulous laugh. 'I feel like I'm doing finger weights, or something.'

'You'll get used to it.' Mateo gestured to the press officer, and he stepped forward. 'Now, the schedule?'

The next ten minutes passed quickly as they rehearsed their brief performance—step out on the balcony, smile and wave, and then Mateo would introduce Rachel as his queen, with their wedding and joint coronation on Saturday to be celebrated as a national holiday.

'That's *insane*,' Rachel murmured, and the press officer gave her an odd look.

'It's quite normal for royal weddings,' Mateo remarked calmly.

'Your Highness, it's time!'

Mateo glanced at Rachel, who had suddenly morphed into the proverbial deer snared by headlights. She threw him a panicked look.

'I can't…'

'You can.' His voice was low and sure as he reached for her hand. 'All you have to do is take a single step, smile and wave.'

She nodded rather frantically. 'Smile and wave. Smile and wave.'

'That's it.'

Two attendants threw open the French windows that led out to the balcony, the massed crowd visible below in a colourful blur.

'Oh, my heavens,' Rachel whispered. 'There are thousands of people down there.'

And even more watching the live video stream, but Mateo chose not to enlighten her.

'Let's do this,' he said, echoing her words from before. She gave him a small smile of recognition, and then he drew her out onto the balcony, the applause crashing over them in a deafening wave as they appeared. He turned to Rachel, his mouth curving in pleasure and pride as she offered the crowds below a radiant smile and a decidedly royal wave.

After a few moments of cheering and clapping, Mateo made his announcement, which was met with even more applause and excited calls. Then a cry rose up: *'Fili! Fili!'*

Rachel's forehead wrinkled slightly as she gave him a questioning look. She didn't know what they were calling for, but Mateo did.

Kiss.

And it seemed like the most natural thing to do, to take her in his arms, her curves fitting snugly against him, and kiss her on the lips.

CHAPTER NINE

RACHEL GAZED DOWN at the list of potential charities to support and marvelled for about the hundredth time that this was now her life.

The last three days had felt like a dream. She had, quite deliberately, chosen to enjoy all the good and ignore the worrisome or flat-out terrifying. And there was a lot of good—not least the people who surrounded her, who were determined to help her to succeed.

The day after her arrival and the announcement on the balcony, Agathe had invited Rachel to her private rooms for breakfast. Eighteen hours later, Rachel's lips had been practically still buzzing from the quick yet thorough kiss Mateo had given her, to the uproarious approval of the crowds below. He'd given her a fleeting, self-satisfied smile afterwards, his eyes glinting with both knowledge and possession, while Rachel had tottered back into the palace on unsteady legs that had had nothing to do with her heels.

She and Agathe had chatted easily over croissants and Greek yogurt withsweet golden honey and slices of succulent melon.

'I can see now more than ever that my son has made a good choice,' Agathe said with a little smile and Rachel blushed as she recalled that kiss yet again.

'It's not like that,' she felt compelled to protest. 'We're only friends. What I mean is, that's all we've been.'

'And it is a good, strong foundation for a marriage. Much better than—' She stopped abruptly, making Rachel frown in confusion.

'Much better than what?' she prompted.

'Oh, you know.' Agathe laughed lightly as she poured them both more of the strong Greek coffee. 'The usual fleeting attraction or empty charm.'

Yet as Agathe dazzled her with a determinedly bright smile, Rachel couldn't shake the feeling that she'd been about to say something else, something she'd decided not to.

Despite that brief moment of awkwardness, the rest of the conversation was easy and comfortable, and Rachel's initial concerns about being intimidated by Mateo's elegant mother proved to be as ill-founded as she might have hoped.

After breakfast, the over-the-top unreality of her situation continued as her personal assistant

Monica—a neatly efficient woman in her late twenties—introduced herself and put herself entirely at Rachel's disposal.

Then came another session with Francesca, who was becoming a firm friend. Rachel knew, despite Mateo's outrage, that the stylist had been merely pragmatic in her assessment of Rachel's looks, although she apologised yet again when they met to discuss her wardrobe, and in particular her evening gown for the ball in a few days' time, and also for her wedding in less than a week.

Rachel's head continued to spin as she was outfitted beyond her wildest imaginings—yet with an eye to what she liked and felt comfortable in. Instead of shapeless trouser suits, she had chic separates in jewel-toned colours that Francesca assured her highlighted her 'flawless skin' and 'gorgeous eyes and hair'. Rachel had never heard herself described in such glowing terms, and some battered part of her that she hadn't let herself acknowledge began to heal…just as it had when Mateo told her she was gorgeous and sexy.

But surely he couldn't have meant that…?

Whether he did or not was not something Rachel let herself dwell on for too long, because either way they were getting married. She'd already told herself she could manage without love, and that included desire, too. At least the kind of head-over-heels, can't-live-without-you desire she knew Mateo didn't feel for her, no matter what he had said.

The trouble was, she felt a little of it for him. Looking at him was starting to send shivery sparks racing along her nerve-endings, and sometimes when she was watching him she had an almost irresistible urge to touch him. Run her hand along the smooth-shaven sleekness of his jaw, or trail her fingertips along the defined pecs she saw beneath the crisp cotton of his shirt.

She didn't, of course, not that she had any opportunity. In the three days since she'd arrived on Kallyria, she'd barely seen Mateo at all. Which was fine, she reminded herself more than once, because he had a country to run and she had a wedding—a whole life—to prepare for.

Rachel made a few ticks next to charities she was interested in supporting before laying the paper aside. She was in her private study, on the ground floor of the palace, a spacious and elegant room with long, sashed windows open to the fragrant gardens outside. Even though it was autumn, the air was still warm, far balmier than the best British summer.

Despite all the beauty and opulence surrounding her, Rachel felt a little flicker of homesickness that she did her best to banish. As wonderful as all this was, as kind as people were, it was still all incredibly unfamiliar. She kept feeling as if she were living someone else's life, and as small as her own had been, at least it had been hers.

At least she'd been able to email her friends and have regular updates about her mother. Her friends had been amazed and thrilled by her change in circumstances; apparently her and Mateo's kiss had been on the cover of several British tabloids. Rachel hadn't felt brave enough to look at any of it online. The thought of seeing herself splashed on the covers of national magazines was both too surreal and scary even to contemplate, much less actually inspect.

Several of her friends and former colleagues from Cambridge were coming to the wedding, all at Mateo's expense, a prospect that lifted her spirits a bit. She wasn't completely cut off from her old life, even if sometimes she felt as if she were.

Rachel rested her chin on her hand as she gazed outside. A bright tropical butterfly landed on a crimson hibiscus blossom, the sight as incredible as anything she might find in the pages of a nature magazine, and yet commonplace in this new world of hers.

She supposed she was bound to feel a bit uncertain and out of sorts, at least at the start. Everything had happened so fast, and the change had been so enormous. She wished she'd seen more of Mateo, because she recognised that he grounded her, and his reassurance would go a long way. But when she'd asked that morning, one of the palace staff had informed her he'd left for the north of the country last night, and wouldn't be back until this evening. He hadn't even told her he was leaving. And she kept telling herself not to mind.

But that didn't mean she had to sit and do nothing about it.

Rachel was busy for the rest of the afternoon, between fittings for her evening gown and wedding dress, and lessons on comportment that Agathe had gently advised her to attend. Rachel hadn't even known what those were until she'd shown up for her first one, and Agathe had begun to explain how to both sit and stand in public; how to make small talk with strangers; how to navigate a table setting with six separate forks, knives, and spoons.

At first Rachel had bristled slightly at the instruction; she wasn't a complete yokel, after all. She knew how to behave in public, surely, and she'd made small talk with plenty of people over her years in academia. Still, it hadn't taken her long to realise, when it came to royalty, she was out of her element, and Agathe was here to help her. She had only a week to become royalty-ready, and she—and Agathe—were determined to make the most of every moment.

As evening fell, the sky scattered with stars, Rachel heard the sound she hadn't even realised she'd been waiting for—the loud, persistent whirr of a helicopter. From the window of her bedroom she watched the royal helicopter touch down on the palace's helipad.

Mateo was back…and she was going to find him.

Mateo scrubbed his gritty eyes as he tried to refocus on the report he was reading. He'd barely slept last night, having spent the last forty-eight hours on the move in the north, trying to arrange a meeting with the leader of the insurgents gathering there.

Despite the unrest, the realisation of his marriage and ascension to the throne had made them more willing to consider a compromise, thank heaven. His marriage to Rachel was already paying dividends.

Rachel. He hadn't seen her in several days, and barely before that. Barely since the kiss on the balcony, when they'd as good as sealed the deal. He wondered how she was now, if she was coping with all the change and busyness. He told himself she was too sensible to have cold feet, but he wished he could see her. He'd make time tomorrow, he promised himself. At least, he'd try to.

A soft footfall outside had him tensing. The

palace was nearly impregnable and teeming with security. He wasn't nervous, not exactly… just conscious that he'd spent the last few days negotiating with desperate men who were little more than terrorists, and if they wanted to put an end to him, before his wedding would be the time to do it.

'Mateo…?' The voice was soft, low, and wonderfully familiar.

'In here.'

The door creaked open and Rachel peeked her head in, smiling with relief when she saw him. 'I've been wandering around in my nightgown, which I realised is probably not the best idea. Certainly not queenly behaviour.'

'Well, you're not a queen yet.' Mateo smiled, pleasure at seeing her like honey in his veins. She was wearing an ivory dressing gown that was all silk and lace and hugged her sweet curves lovingly.

She caught him looking at her and, grimacing, spread her arms wide. 'Isn't this the most ridiculous thing ever? Francesca insists it's perfectly appropriate night-time attire for a queen, but I feel a bit like—I don't know—Lady Godiva.'

'As I recall, Lady Godiva was meant to be naked, as well as on a horse.'

'Right.' Rachel laughed huskily. 'Well, you know what I mean.'

Yes, he did. Just as he knew that with the lamplight behind her and her arms spread, Rachel might as well be naked. Out of decency he knew he should inform her of the fact, but he didn't want to embarrass her—and he was enjoying the view.

'Anyway.' She dropped her arms and moved towards him, so the robe became seemly again, more was the pity. 'Where have you been? How *are* you? I haven't seen you since—well, since the balcony.'

She blushed at that, which Mateo liked. He might have been trying to keep Rachel at arm's length, but the memory of that kiss was scorched onto his brain. And after several days of having her much farther away than his arm, he was enjoying her company far too much to put up the usual barriers.

'I know, I'm sorry. I'm afraid I have had much to command my attention.'

'You don't have to apologise.' She perched on the edge of his desk, giving him a small smile. 'You were up north?'

'Trying to set up some peace talks, yes.'

'And were you successful?'

'I believe so.'

'And now?' She nodded towards the stack of files on his desk. 'What are you working on now?'

He paused, because he had already developed

the instinct to keep his royal work private, and yet this was the woman he'd hashed out every potential problem with for a decade. They'd wrangled and wrestled with countless theorems and difficulties, had debated the best way forward on countless experiments, had worked side by side most days. He'd wanted to marry her for just those reasons, and yet sharing this work did not come naturally to him.

'Mateo?'

'I'm trying to decide who to place in my cabinet of ministers,' he said at last. 'When a new king ascends to the throne, it is his privilege and right to choose his own cabinet.'

'Is it? That's a lot of power to hand to one person.'

'Indeed, but his choices must be ratified by sixty per cent of parliament, which helps to keep things balanced.'

'So what's the problem?'

Mateo gestured to the stack of files, each one containing information on potential ministers. 'I don't actually know any of these people. I've been away from Kallyria for too long.' He could not keep the recrimination from his voice. This was his fault.

'Then you can get to know them, surely.' Rachel edged closer, so her hip was brushing Mateo's hand. She leaned over so she could glance at the files, and gave him a delightful view down the front of her dressing gown.

'I can, but it's a matter of time. I need things settled and stabilised as quickly as possible.' With what was surely a herculean effort, he dragged his gaze away from Rachel's front.

'You must have some top contenders.' She reached for the first file, her narrowed gaze scanning it quickly. Mateo leaned back and watched her work, enjoying the sight—her hair spilling over her shoulders, her breasts nearly spilling out of her nightgown. He could practically hear her brain ticking over. Smart *and* sexy.

'You're looking at one of them.'

'Mm.' She continued to read the file before tossing it aside. 'No.'

'No?' Mateo repeated in surprise. 'Why not?'

'Look at his voting pattern.' She gestured to the third sheet of the file. 'Entirely inconsistent. He can't be trusted.'

Mateo leaned forward to glance at the relevant part of the document. 'I wouldn't say it's entirely inconsistent. I think it was more of knowing which way the wind was blowing.'

'You want people with principles. Otherwise they will be swayed—sometimes by you, and sometimes not.'

'True,' Mateo acknowledged. He realised how much he appreciated her input, and how much he was enjoying the sight of her. 'What about the next one?'

Over the next few hours, they went through every single file, creating piles of yes, maybe, and definitely not. Mateo was grateful for Rachel's input, and as they discussed the different candidates they fell into a familiar pattern of bouncing ideas off one another, along with the banter between them that he'd always enjoyed.

'You just like him because he went to Cambridge,' Rachel scoffed. 'You are so biased.'

'And you're not?'

'Of course not.' She smiled at him, chocolate eyes glinting, and quite suddenly as well as quite absolutely, Mateo found he had to kiss her.

'Come here,' he said softly, and Rachel's eyes widened as he reached for the sash of her robe and tugged on it.

'I'm afraid that's not going to do it,' she said with a husky laugh. 'Silk isn't strong enough.'

'But I am.' He anchored his hands on her hips as he pulled her towards him—and she came, a little breathlessly, a little nervously, but she came.

Mateo settled her on his lap, enjoying the soft, silky armful of her. Her hair brushed his jaw as she placed her hands tentatively on his shoulders.

'This feels a bit weird,' she whispered.

He chuckled. 'Good weird or bad weird?'

'Oh, definitely good.' Her anxious gaze scanned his face. 'Don't you think?'

'I definitely think,' Mateo murmured, 'that we should stop talking.'

Rachel's mouth snapped shut and Mateo angled his head so his lips were a breath away from hers. He could feel her tremble. 'Don't you think?' he whispered.

'Oh, um, yes.'

That was all he needed to settle his mouth on hers, her lips parting softly as a sigh of pleasure escaped her. Her hands clenched on his shoulders and he drew her closer so he could feel the delicious press of her breasts against his chest.

He deepened the kiss, sweeping his tongue inside the velvet softness of her mouth. She let out a little mewl, which enflamed his senses all the more. The need to kiss her became the need to possess her, with an urgency that raced through his veins and turned his insides to fire.

He slid his hand along the silky length of her thigh, spreading her legs so she was straddling him, the softest part of her pressed hard against his arousal. He flexed his hips instinctively, and she moaned against his mouth and pressed back.

He was going to explode. Literally. Figuratively. In every way possible. Mateo pressed against her once more as his brain blurred. Her hands were like claws on his shoulders, her breasts flattened against his chest. He slid his hands under her robe to fill them with those generous curves, everything in him short-circuiting.

If he didn't stop this now, he was going to humiliate himself—and her. They couldn't have their wedding night in a *chair.*

Gasping, he tore his mouth away from hers and with shaky hands set her back on the desk. Her lips were swollen from his kisses, her hair in a dark tangle about her flushed face, her nightgown in delicious disarray. Mateo dragged his hands through his hair as he sought to calm his breathing.

'We need to stop.'

'Do we?' Rachel asked shakily. She pulled her robe closed, her fingers trembling.

'Yes. This isn't…' He shook his head, appalled at how affected he was. The blood was still roaring through his veins, and he most definitely needed an ice-cold shower. He couldn't remember the last time he'd felt this way about a woman.

Yes, you can.

Abruptly he rose from the chair and stalked to the window, his back to Rachel. 'I'm sorry,' he managed to choke out. 'I shouldn't have taken such advantage.'

'Was that what you were doing?' Rachel asked with a husky yet uncertain laugh.

'We're not married yet,' Mateo stated flatly.

'I'm a grown-up, Mateo, and we're getting married in three days. I think it was allowed.' She sounded wry, but also confused. He still couldn't look at her.

Their relationship wasn't supposed to be like this. Yes, he enjoyed their camaraderie, and the physical attraction was an added bonus he hadn't expected. But the way his need for her had consumed him? The way it had obliterated all rational thought?

No, that wasn't something he was willing to feel. He could not sacrifice his self-control to his marriage.

'You should go to bed,' he said, his voice brusque, and a long silence ensued. He waited, not willing to turn, and then finally he heard the swish of silk as she slid off the table.

'Goodnight, Mateo,' she said softly, and then he heard the click of the door closing as she left the room.

CHAPTER TEN

RACHEL GAZED AT her reflection anxiously as the flurry of nerves in her stomach threatened to make their way up her throat. In just fifteen minutes she was going to enter the palace ballroom on Mateo's arm, and be presented to all Kallyrian society as his bride-to-be.

Their wedding was in less than forty-eight hours, a fact that kept bouncing off Rachel's brain, refusing to penetrate. In forty-eight hours they would be *married*, and then crowned King and Queen in a joint ceremony.

A fact which would have filled her with excitement last night, when she and Mateo had worked together on the list of potential cabinet ministers, and then he'd kissed her.

Oh, how he'd kissed her. Rachel had never been kissed like that in her life, and she'd been in a ferment of desire since, longing to be kissed again—and more. So much more. To feel his hands on her, his mouth possessing her, his gloriously hard body beneath her…

But since he'd rather unceremoniously pushed her off his lap, Mateo had avoided her like the proverbial plague. At least, it felt that way. Rachel told herself he had to be busy, but she knew it was more than that, after the way he'd ended their kiss and turned his back, quite literally, to her.

She had no idea what had made him back off so abruptly, but the fact that he had filled her with both disappointment and fear. Was she a clumsy kisser? Heaven knew, it was perfectly possible. It wasn't as if she'd had loads of experience. Or maybe he'd gone off her for some reason—when he'd touched her? She knew she was a little overweight. Maybe Mateo now knew it too.

The thought made her stomach clench as she frowned at her reflection, all her old insecurities, the ones she'd fought so hard to master, rising up in her again. Whatever it was, he'd ended the kiss and then avoided her ever since, so she hadn't seen him from that moment to this. At least, she hoped she'd see him in this moment—they were meant to enter the ball together, after all, in just a few minutes.

Taking a deep breath, Rachel ran her hands down the sides of her gown, a fairy-tale dress if there ever was one. Made of bronze silk, it was strapless with a nipped-in waist and a delightfully full skirt that shimmered every time she moved. The dress was complemented with a parure from the Kallyrian crown jewels—a tiara made of topaz and diamonds, with a matching necklace, bracelet, and teardrop diamond earrings. She truly was Cinderella; the only question was when and if midnight would strike.

A knock sounded on the door of her bedroom, and, with her heart fluttering along with her nerves, Rachel croaked, 'Come in.'

The door opened and Mateo stood there, looking devastatingly handsome in white tie and tails. They were the perfect foil for his olive skin and black hair, his eyes an impossibly bright blue-green in his tanned face.

'Well?' Rachel asked shakily as she straightened her shoulders. 'Will I do?'

'You look stunning.' The compliment, delivered with such quiet sincerity, made a lump form in her throat.

Why did you push me away? She longed to ask, but didn't dare. She wasn't brave or strong enough to hear the answer.

'These jewels are stunning,' she said, nervously touching one of her earrings. 'When Francesca showed them to me, I couldn't believe I was meant to wear them.'

'Who else should wear them?' Mateo countered. 'You are Queen.'

'Technically, I'm not. Not for another forty-eight hours.'

'It is as good as done. Tonight, in the eyes of the world, you are my Queen.'

Rachel shook her head slowly. 'I feel like I'm living in a dream.'

'Is that a bad thing?' Mateo asked, his gaze fastened on hers.

'No, but the thing with dreams is…you have to wake up.'

'Maybe with this one you don't. Maybe it will go on for ever.'

She laughed uncertainly. 'No dream lasts for ever, Mateo.'

He acknowledged her point with a nod. 'True.'

What, Rachel wondered, were they really talking about? She felt an undercurrent to their conversation, to the tension tautening the air between them. He extended his hand, and she took it, the feel of his warm, dry palm under hers sending little shocks along her arm. She would never stop responding to him, and yet it seemed he could turn his physical response to her off like a tap.

She pushed the thought away. She had enough insecurity to deal with already, appearing in public, knowing there would be whispers and rumours, criticisms as well as compliments. It was the nature of being a public figure, which, amazingly, she had now become.

'Ready?' Mateo asked softly, and she nodded.

They walked in silence from her bedroom in the palace's east wing, along the plushly carpeted corridor to the double staircase that led down to the palace's main entrance hall. The hall had been cleared for their entrance, save for a few security men flanking the doors to the ballroom, where a thousand guests were waiting.

Dizziness assailed Rachel and she nearly stumbled in the heels she still wasn't used to wearing.

'Breathe,' Mateo murmured, his hand steady on her elbow.

'You try breathing when you're wearing knickers that are nearly cutting you in half,' Rachel returned tartly, and was gratified to see his mouth quirk in a smile. No matter how Mateo did or did not feel about her physically, Rachel didn't want to lose his friendship. As he'd said before, it was a good foundation for a marriage. She needed to remember that. She needed to remind herself of how important it was.

'Here we go,' Mateo said, and two white-gloved footmen opened the double doors to the ballroom. Taking a deep breath, Rachel held her head high as she sailed into the room on Mateo's arm.

The crowd in the ballroom parted like the Red Sea as they entered under the glittering lights of a dozen chandeliers. The guests naturally formed an aisle that Mateo and Rachel walked down, hands linked and held aloft.

'We'll have to dance,' Mateo murmured. 'The first waltz. It is expected.'

'Dance?' Rachel whispered back as she nearly tripped on the trailing hem of her gown. 'No one told me that! I don't dance.'

'It's a simple box step. Follow my lead and you'll be fine.' They were almost at the end of the aisle, and panic was icing Rachel's insides.

'No, really,' she said out of the side of her mouth, her gaze still straight ahead. She felt like a bad ventriloquist. 'I. Don't. Dance. At *all*. Two left feet would be a kind way of putting it.'

Why hadn't Agathe covered this in her comportment lessons? Or had she just assumed that Rachel could dance?

She risked a glance at Mateo's face; he wore the faint smile he'd had on since they'd entered the ballroom. He was so handsome it hurt. And she was about to humiliate herself publicly in front of a thousand people, and, really, the whole world. She was wearing a dress worthy of Beauty in *Beauty and the Beast*, but in this case she felt like the beast.

'Mateo—'

'Just follow my lead.'

'I *can't*—'

'Trust me.' The two words, simply spoken and

heartfelt, were enough to allay her fears, or almost. Whatever he had planned, she knew she would follow along.

The crowds parted to reveal an empty expanse of gleaming parquet, a string orchestra poised at the other end. As Mateo escorted her to the centre of the floor, they struck up a familiar waltz tune: 'Gold and Silver'.

Rachel stared at him in blind panic.

'Put your feet on top of mine,' Mateo murmured, so low she almost didn't hear the words.

'On top? I'll kill your feet—'

'Do it.'

She did, and Mateo didn't even wince as she practically crushed his toes.

'Hold on,' he said, slipping one hand around her waist, and the next thing Rachel knew she was flying around the dance floor, her skirt swinging out in an elegant bell as Mateo moved them both around in a perfectly elegant waltz.

'Are you in agony?' she whispered as he arced around, carrying her easily without even seeming to do it.

'Smile.'

She did. Two more minutes of soaring music and graceful moves when she felt as if she were flying, and then finally, thankfully, the waltz was over. The crowd erupted into applause and Mateo looked at Rachel and winked.

* * *

His feet were killing him, it was true, but the sight of Rachel looking at him in wonder and admiration and maybe even something more made it worth it. More than worth it. The look she gave him could have powered a city. Or perhaps the feeling inside him could have.

Whatever it was, Mateo felt like a king—of the whole world.

'Your Highness.' A local dignitary, someone whose name Mateo had forgotten, approached him with a bow. 'That was exceptional. Please let me introduce you to my wife…'

The next hour passed in a blur of introductions and small talk. Just as he'd known she would, Rachel shone. She wasn't one to give tinkling laughs or arch looks; she was far too genuine for that. But she talked to everyone as if she wanted to, and she listened as if she was really interested in what they had to say. Mateo was proud to have her on his arm and, more importantly, she seemed happy to be there. The evening, he knew, would be deemed a great success.

He didn't think anything of it when Rachel was escorted into dinner by Lukas Diakis, a senior minister from his father's cabinet. Nor when she listened politely to his Aunt Karolina, her gaze darting occasionally to him. He smiled back every time, but her own smiles became smaller and smaller until they were barely a stretching of his lips, and then they weren't there at all, because she'd stopped looking at him.

Mateo told himself not to be concerned. What on earth could a doddering retired minister or an elderly spinster aunt possibly say to Rachel to make her seem so thoughtful and pale?

Still Mateo couldn't shake his unease through the six-course meal. Even though they were at opposite ends of the table, he felt her disquiet. Or was he just being fanciful? It wasn't as if they had some sort of mental or, heaven forbid, emotional connection. He didn't even want that.

At the end of the meal Rachel left first, arm in arm with Diakis. Mateo watched them go, but by the time he'd made it back to the ballroom she was lost in the crowd and annoyance bit at him. She was his wife. He'd already told her they would spend much of the evening apart, mingling and chatting, but now he wanted her by his side.

He needed her there, which would have alarmed him except right now he didn't care. He just wanted to find her.

Another hour of mingling passed, endless and interminable. Occasionally Mateo glimpsed Rachel across the room, but it would have been impolite, if not downright impossible, to storm through the crowds and approach her. Besides, as the minutes ran into hours, Mateo managed to convince himself that nothing was amiss…and he certainly didn't *need* anything or anyone. He breathed a sigh of relief at the thought.

Finally the evening came to an end. It was two in the morning, the sky full of stars, as the guests departed in a laughing stream, while Mateo, Rachel, and his mother all stood by the door, saying their official farewells. Rachel looked ready to wilt.

'Such a success!' Agathe kissed Rachel on both cheeks. 'You were marvellous, my dear. Absolutely marvellous.' She turned to Mateo. 'Wasn't it a success, Mateo? An absolute triumph!'

'It was.' He glanced searchingly at Rachel, but her gaze flitted away. What was going on?

'I must say goodnight,' Agathe said on a sigh. 'I am absolutely exhausted, as you both must be.' She kissed Mateo's cheek. 'You've done so well.'

'Thank you, Mitera.'

His mother headed upstairs, and the staff melted away to clean up after the ball. They were alone in the great entrance hall, the space stretching into shadows under the dimmed lights of the chandelier high above. From outside someone laughed, and a car door slammed before an engine purred away.

'You really were wonderful,' Mateo told her.

'Your feet must be killing you.' Rachel reached up and took out the teardrop earrings. 'These are lovely, but they're agony to wear. I haven't worn earrings since my uni days.'

'You look amazing.'

'Thank you.' She still wasn't looking at him, and Mateo bit back his annoyance. What game was she playing?

'I think I'll go to bed.' Rachel let out a little laugh that sounded brittle as she started towards the staircase. 'I think I could fall asleep right here.'

'It's been a long evening.'

'Yes.' She glanced back at him, like a beautiful flame in her bronze gown with the topazes and diamonds glinting in her hair and at her throat and wrists. 'Goodnight, Mateo.' She almost sounded sad, and that irritated him further. They'd had a brilliant evening, they were getting married the day after tomorrow, and she was playing some passive-aggressive game of showing him she was sad without actually saying it.

'Why don't you just tell me what's going on, Rachel?' His voice came out hard, harder than he'd meant it to, but he'd never liked these games. Not with Cressida, when he'd so often had to guess the reason for her pique, and not with Rachel. Not with anyone.

Her eyes widened as she stilled, one hand on the banister. 'What...what do you mean?'

'You know what I mean.'

She stiffened, her eyes flashing with affront at his tone. 'I really don't.'

'Are you sure about that?' Mateo knew he was handling this all wrong, but hours of wondering and worrying that something was amiss had strung him tighter than he'd realised. He was ready to snap now, and it was hard to pull back.

'Yes, I'm quite sure. I'm tired, Mateo, and I want to go to bed.'

So he should let her go. He knew that, and yet somehow he couldn't. 'Why did you keep giving me looks all evening?'

'Looks?'

'During dinner. As if…' He struggled to put a name to the expression in her eyes. 'As if you were disappointed in me.' The realisation that that was indeed what her look had been was a heaviness in his gut.

Recognition flashed in Rachel's eyes, and Mateo knew he was right. Something was wrong…and she didn't want to tell him what it was. She wanted him to guess, and beg, and plead. He'd been here before, and he hated it. He wouldn't play that game.

'You know what? Never mind.' He shook his head, the movement abrupt, dismissive. 'I don't care what it is. If you can't be bothered to tell me, I can't be bothered to find out.'

'Why are you so angry?' She sounded bewildered, and rightly so. He was overreacting, he knew it, and yet he still couldn't keep himself from it. Because this was bringing back too many old, painful memories, memories he'd suppressed for fifteen years. He really didn't want them rising up now.

'I'm not angry.' His tone made his words a lie.

She gave a little shrug, as if the point wasn't worth arguing, which it probably wasn't. His hands balled into fists at his sides.

'Rachel…'

'Fine, Mateo, if you want to do this now.' She let out a weary sigh that shuddered through her whole body before she gave him a look that was both direct and sorrowful. 'Who is Cressida?'

CHAPTER ELEVEN

SHE HADN'T WANTED to confront him. She'd told herself there was no point. And yet Mateo had forced an argument, much to her own shock, because he'd never acted in such an emotional and unreasonable way before. And now they were here, and she'd asked the question that had been burning on her tongue since Karolina had patted her hand at dinner and said in a dreamy way, *'You're so much better for him than Cressida, my dear.'*

When Rachel had smiled politely in return, the conversation had moved on, but then the man who had escorted her from the table had said something similar.

'Thank God he didn't marry Cressida.'

And Rachel had started to feel…unmoored. She couldn't have explained it better than that, that the sudden emergence of this unknown woman that Mateo must have considered marrying had left her feeling entirely and unsettlingly adrift. And so she'd asked, and now she wasn't sure she wanted to know the answer.

Who is Cressida?

Mateo stared at her unsmilingly, his hands still in fists by his sides. 'Where did you hear that name?' he asked tonelessly, but with a seething undercurrent of anger that Rachel sensed all the way from the stairs.

'Does it matter?'

'Where?'

She stiffened at his tone. She'd never seen Mateo like this, and it frightened her. It made her wonder if she knew him at all.

Who *was* Cressida?

Did she really want to know?

'Karolina told me,' she said. 'And then Lukas Diakis, the minister.'

'What did they say?'

She stared at him, willing the fierce mask to crack. Why was he looking so terribly ferocious? She shrugged, deciding to play it straight, as she played everything. She was never one for machinations, manipulations, a sly tone, a leading question, no matter what Mateo had just accused her of.

'Karolina said she thought I was better for you than Cressida, and Lukas said he was glad you didn't marry her.' Mateo's face darkened, his brows drawing together in a black slash. Rachel took a step backwards on the stairs and nearly stumbled on her gown.

'They should not have spoken of her.'

His icy tone should have kept her from saying anything, but Rachel sensed that if they didn't talk about Cressida now, they never would.

'Who is she, Mateo? Why have you never mentioned her before?'

'Why should I have?'

'She's obviously someone important to you.' Rachel struggled to keep her tone reasonable even though she had an almost uncontrollable urge to burst into tears.

It was past two in the morning, she'd had the longest and most stressful night of her life, wonderful as it had been, and she knew she was feeling far too fragile to handle a big discussion right now…just as she knew they needed to have it.

'You dated her,' she said, making it not quite a question.

'Yes.' Mateo's mouth thinned to a hard, unforgiving line. 'It was a long time ago. It's not important.'

Not important? Was he serious?

'She seemed like someone important to you, judging from your reaction now.'

'My reaction,' Mateo informed her in as chilly a tone as she'd ever heard from him, 'was because my relatives and civil servants were gossiping about me like a bunch of fishwives.'

'It wasn't like that—'

'It was exactly like that.' Mateo strode past her, up the stairs. Rachel watched him go with a sense of incredulity. This was so unlike Mateo, it was almost funny. He wasn't this cold, autocratic, ridiculous dictator of a man. He just *wasn't*.

And yet right now he was.

'Why won't you tell me about her, Mateo?' she called up the stairs. 'We're about to be *married*—'

He did not break his stride as he answered. 'It is not to be discussed.'

Rachel watched him disappear up the stairs, dazed by how quickly things had spiralled out of control. Alone in the soaring entrance hall, she strained her ears to hear the distant sound of Mateo's bedroom door closing.

She glanced around the empty hall and swallowed hard. She felt numb inside, too numb to cry. Had they just had their first argument?

Or their last?

Slowly she walked up the stairs. She was still in her gown and jewels, but the clock had definitely struck midnight. The party was over.

Francesca was waiting for her in her bedroom, eager to hear about the party as she helped her undress.

'You wowed them all, I am sure,' she exclaimed. 'So beautiful…'

Rachel forced a smile as she bent her head and allowed Francesca to undo the clasp of her necklace. She remained quiet as she took off the rest of her jewels, and the stylist put them away in a black velvet case that would be returned directly to the vault where all the crown jewels were kept.

Then Francesca undid the zip of her gown, and Rachel carefully stepped out of it, and into the waiting robe.

'I drew you a bath,' Francesca said as she swathed the dress in a protective bag. 'I know it's late, but I thought you might want to relax.'

'Thank you, Francesca, you're a saint.' Since their first meeting, when Mateo had glowered at and almost fired her, Francesca had proved to be a stalwart stylist and a good friend. Rachel was grateful for the other woman's support.

With the dress draped over one arm, Francesca frowned at her. 'Is everything all right?'

Rachel managed another wan smile. 'Just tired. Exhausted, really.' She considered asking Francesca if she knew who Cressida was, but she could imagine Mateo's reaction if he discovered she was asking around. Clearly, for him, the woman was off-limits to everyone, even Rachel. Especially Rachel.

'Have a bath and get some sleep,' Francesca advised. 'It's a big day tomorrow.'

'Another one?' Every day had been a big day.

'We have the final fitting for your dress, a rehearsal for the ceremony, and a dinner in the evening with about thirty guests.'

Rachel's head drooped at the thought of it. 'Right. Okay.'

'You're sure everything is all right?' Francesca looked at her, worry clouding her eyes.

For a second Rachel wanted to confide in the other woman. She wanted to confess to all the doubts that were now crowding her heart and mind.

I don't know if I can cope with this. I'm not sure I'm queen material after all. I'm afraid the man I'm about to marry is still in love with another woman.

'I'm fine,' Rachel said as firmly as she could. 'Thank you.'

Francesca patted her on the shoulder and left the room, and Rachel sagged visibly once the woman had gone, unable to put up a front any longer.

She nearly fell asleep in the bath, the hot water doing its best to loosen the knots tightening her shoulder blades. When she finally got out of the bathroom, dripping wet and aching with both tiredness and sorrow, she fell across the bed, pulling the duvet across her, her hair still in a wet tangle, and didn't stir until bright autumn sunshine was pouring through the windows whose shutters she'd forgotten to close.

In the morning light, everything seemed a little better. At least, Rachel felt more resolved. Last night she'd been blindsided by Mateo's sudden change in attitude, the way he'd morphed from the charming, easy-going man she'd known into some parody of a cold, frosty stranger. She knew the pressures of his kingship weighed on him heavily, but he'd never taken that tone with her before, and Rachel had no intention of setting some sort of awful precedent now.

She showered and dressed, blow-dried her hair into artful waves and chose one of her new outfits to boost her confidence—a pair of wide-leg trousers and a cowl-necked topped in soft maroon jersey. Her engagement ring glinted as she moved, reminding her of the promises they'd already made to each other. They'd get through this. They were getting married tomorrow, after all.

Finding Mateo, however, was not as easy as Rachel hoped. After a buffet breakfast in the palace dining room by herself, she was whisked away by Monica, her personal assistant, to the final fitting of her wedding gown.

Rachel loved the pure simplicity of the white

silk gown, with its edging of antique lace on the sleeves and hem, and the long veil of matching lace. When she wore it, she truly felt like a princess. A queen.

After the fitting, Monica met with her in the study Rachel was to call her own, going over the schedule of events on tomorrow's big day. Rachel scanned down the list—wedding ceremony and coronation in the cathedral across the square, and then a walkabout through the plaza to greet well-wishers before returning to the palace for a wedding breakfast. Then a turn around the city in a horse and carriage before returning to the palace for a ball, and finally spending their wedding night there in a private suite. Considering Mateo's responsibilities, there would be no honeymoon.

'That looks like a very full day,' Rachel said with a smile, trying to ignore the butterflies swarming in her middle. Even though she was getting a little bit used to being in the public eye, the thought of all those events made her feel dizzy with anxiety. What if she tripped and fell flat on her face? What if she was sick? Considering how nervous she was, she knew it was perfectly possible. She could utterly humiliate herself in front of thousands of people, not to mention those watching from their homes, since everything was to be broadcast live.

Don't think about it, she instructed herself.

When the times comes, you'll just do it. You'll have to.

She turned to Monica with as bright a smile as she could manage. 'Do you know where the king is?'

The wind streamed by him, making his eyes water, as Mateo bent low over the horse and gave it its head. The world was a blur of sea, sand, and sky as the stallion raced over the dunes.

When he'd woken up that morning after a few hours of restless sleep, he'd known he needed to get out of the palace. Out of his own head. And riding one of the many horses in the royal stables was the perfect way to do it.

Mateo hadn't been on a horse in years, but as soon as he'd settled himself atop Mesonyktio, the Greek word for midnight, he'd felt as if he were coming home. And feeling the world fall away, even if just for a few minutes, was a blessed and much-needed relief.

He was still angry with himself for the way he'd handled the altercation with Rachel. He was also angry with his meddling relatives and colleagues for mentioning Cressida; he'd only brought her to Kallyria once, fifteen years ago, but they remembered.

He remembered. He'd been so besotted. So

sure that she was the only, the ultimate, woman for him.

Of course she hadn't been. His gut tightened and he leaned farther over Mesonyktio's head, letting the wind and speed chase away the last of his tumultuous thoughts.

By the time he arrived back at the stables, he was tired enough not to have to think too much about last night, or how he regretted the way he'd handled that tense and unexpected situation with Rachel.

He slid off Mesonyktio's back and led him by the reins into the dim coolness of the palace stables, only to stiffen when he heard a familiar voice say quietly, 'Mateo.'

He blinked in the gloom, breathing in the smell of horse and hay, and then focused his gaze on Rachel, standing in front of him, chin tilted, eyes direct.

'What are you doing here?'

'I wanted to talk to you.'

He drew a deep breath, forcing himself to relax. 'All right. Let me see to the horse first.'

She nodded and stepped out of the way as he brought Mesonyktio to his stall and began to unfasten his saddle.

'I didn't even know you rode.'

'Not much time or space for it, back in Cambridge.'

'No, I suppose not.'

She remained quiet as he rubbed the horse down, taking his time to delay the moment when he'd have to face her. He should apologise. He knew that. Yet somehow the words wouldn't come.

Finally there was nothing more to do with Mesonyktio, and Mateo knew he could not delay the inevitable. He turned around and faced his bride-to-be. She looked lovely in a pair of tailored trousers and a soft top in burgundy that made the most of her curves. Her hair was loose about her shoulders, her eyes wide and dark and fastened on him.

'I want to talk about last night,' she said without preamble. Rachel was no shrinking violet, never had been. She had always been willing to be confrontational at work, politely so, but still. Mateo should have known she wouldn't let last night go, no matter how foreboding he might have seemed.

'I'm sorry if I seemed a bit abrupt,' he said. 'It's a sensitive subject.'

Her eyebrows rose. 'You seemed a bit abrupt? Nice try, Mateo, but I'm not having that.'

Despite the tension coiling inside him, he almost smiled. 'You're not?'

'No. We're about to be married.' She glanced at her watch, an elegant strip of diamond-encrusted gold that was part of her trousseau. 'In less than twenty-four hours. I'm not having you go all glowery on me and refuse to discuss something that is clearly important. The whole point of marrying me, or so you said, was because we were friends, and we liked and trusted one another. So don't pull the Scary King act on me, okay?'

'I don't think "glowery" is actually a word.'

'Well, it should be. And if it was in the dictionary, you'd be next to the definition.' She blew out a breath. 'So, look. Just tell me what the deal with Cressida is.'

Even now, when she'd played her hand straight, the way she always did, he was reluctant to reveal the truth, and what details he gave her he would do so sparingly.

'I told you all you need to know, Rachel. I dated her back in university. We were both young. The relationship ended.'

'There must be more to it than that.'

'I don't ask you about your relationship with that man who broke your heart,' he retorted, and she flinched.

'He didn't break my heart. I told you that. I said I was never in love with him.' She paused, seeming to weigh whether she wanted to ask the question he already knew was coming. 'Were you in love with her? Cressida?'

Mateo stood still, doing his best to keep his face bland, his body relaxed. It took effort. 'I suppose I was. Yes.'

She nodded slowly, as if absorbing a blow. 'I wish you had told me before.'

'Before? When, exactly?'

'When you asked me to marry you.' A crumpled note of hurt entered her voice, and she took a breath, clearly striving to hold onto her composure.

'Would it have made a difference?'

'I don't know, but you know as well as I do, Mateo, that when a scientist does not have all the relevant information regarding an experiment, they cannot draw an accurate conclusion.'

Mateo folded his arms and attempted to stare her down. He should have known he wouldn't succeed. Rachel had never been one to be cowed. 'What happened before has no relevance on the present or the future, Rachel. Our future. It was a long time ago. Fifteen years.'

'Yet you can't say her name,' she said softly. 'You haven't said it once since we've started talking about her.'

Everything in him tightened. 'I admit, it was a painful time. I do not wish to revisit it.'

'So fifteen years on, you still have trouble speaking about it? About her?' She shook her head sorrowfully. 'That does make a difference, Mateo.'

'Why?' he demanded. 'It ended a long time ago, Rachel. It doesn't matter any more.'

'Is she the reason you want a loveless marriage?' Rachel asked stonily.

'I didn't say that—'

'You as good as did. One based on friendship and trust, rather than love. That's been clear all along, Mateo. You told me you weren't interested in falling in love. I just… I didn't realise it was because you'd been in love before.'

He flinched at that, but did not deny it.

'So.' Rachel nodded slowly. 'That's how it is.'

'This really doesn't need to change things, Rachel. Like I said, it was a long time ago.'

'What happened?' Rachel asked. 'I deserve to know that much. How did it end? Did she leave you?'

Mateo struggled to keep his expression even, his voice neutral. 'She died.'

'Oh.' The sound that escaped her was soft and sad. 'I'm so sorry.' He nodded jerkily, not willing to say more. To reveal more. 'So if she hadn't died…' Rachel said quietly, almost to herself, and Mateo did not finish that thought. She nodded again, then looked up at him. 'You should have told me,' she stated quietly. 'No matter how long ago it happened. I should have known.'

'I didn't realise it mattered.'

'Then you are not nearly as emotionally astute as I thought you were,' she retorted with dignity.

'You talked about how you trusted me, Mateo, but what about whether I can trust you?'

'This is not about trust—'

'Isn't it?' The two words were quiet and sad, and she didn't wait for his answer as she walked out of the stables.

CHAPTER TWELVE

TODAY WAS HER wedding day. Rachel gazed into the mirror at her princess-like reflection and tried to banish the foreboding that fell over her like a dark cloud.

Ever since her confrontation with Mateo in the stables yesterday, she'd felt as if she were walking under it, blundering forward in a storm of uncertainty, trying to make peace with this new knowledge of her husband-to-be, and what it might mean for their marriage.

So he'd had his heart broken. He'd been deeply in love with a woman, and she'd died. It wasn't a deal-breaker, surely, but Rachel would have appreciated knowing and adjusting to the fact before she was about to walk down the aisle.

No matter what Mateo might insist, it made a difference knowing he'd loved and lost rather than believing he'd never been interested in loving at all.

All through yesterday, as she'd gone through

the motions of their wedding rehearsal, and chatted over dinner with dignitaries whose names she couldn't remember, a battle had been raging in her head.

Should I? Shouldn't I?

But at the end of the day, when she'd gone up to her suite of rooms and seen her wedding gown swathed in plastic and ready for her to wear in the morning, she'd known there wasn't a battle at all.

Her wedding was the next day. Her marriage was already set in motion. She had a *coin* with her name minted on it, as Mateo had informed her that evening. She couldn't walk away from this, just because the situation was a little bit messier than she'd anticipated. There was far, far more riding on this marriage than her own happiness.

And yet…it caused a pain like grief deep inside her to know that Mateo had loved another woman, loved her enough to not want to love someone else ever again. It was, she told herself, a grief she could get used to, and would ultimately have to live with, but a grief, nonetheless.

Since their confrontation in the stables, Rachel had felt a coolness between her and Mateo that definitely hadn't been there before, and it saddened her. It was no way to start a marriage, to say vows, with this tension between them.

And yet that was how it seemed it was going to be.

She'd woken that morning to bright sunshine and pealing bells—apparently they would ring all morning, until the wedding. Rachel tried to tune them out as Francesca helped her dress, giving her understated make-up and sweeping her hair into an elegant up-do.

'This feels crazy,' Rachel murmured numbly as she stood in front of the mirror and gazed at the vision she beheld. 'That can't be me.'

'It is,' Francesca said with a wide smile. 'You look utterly fabulous.'

'All thanks to you.'

'Not all,' the stylist answered with a wink. 'But I'll take a *tiny* bit of credit.'

Rachel moved to the window that overlooked the front of the palace and the large square that stretched to the cathedral on the other side, already crowded with spectators even though it was still several hours until the ceremony.

Many looked as if they had set up early, with camping chairs and flasks of coffee, and others were waving flags or banners. All for her...her and Mateo.

Since coming to Kallyria, Rachel had been too busy and overwhelmed to look online and find out what the media was saying about her and Mateo, and in truth she wasn't sure she wanted to know. Now, however, as she eyed a banner that said simply *True Love*, she wondered.

'Francesca,' she asked slowly. 'What are they saying about Mateo and me?'

The stylist, who was tidying away the many cosmetics she'd used to create Rachel's natural look, glanced up with an arched eyebrow. 'Hmm?'

'What are they saying about us? Are they asking why we're marrying?' Rachel caught sight of a sign that read *A Real-life Fairy Tale*!

'Well…' Francesca paused as she mentally reviewed all she'd heard and read. 'Nothing bad, if you're worried about that. Everyone thinks it's incredibly romantic that you've worked together for so long and that now he's king Mateo wants you by his side. I mean, it *is* romantic, right?'

Rachel forced her lips upwards in what she suspected was a parody of a smile. 'Right.'

'I mean, Mateo could have chosen anyone… but he wanted you. People are saying you're the luckiest woman in the world.'

'Right,' Rachel said again. She turned back to the window, not wanting Francesca to see the expression on her face.

The luckiest woman in the world.

Why did she not feel that way right now? Why did she feel as if she were living a lie?

A short while later, it was time to go. Francesca arranged her veil to spread out behind her as

Rachel headed down the staircase to the palace's entrance hall, for a round of official photographs.

Her cheeks ached from smiling, and the heavy satin of the dress felt as if it was weighing her down, as Rachel posed for photograph after photograph. This was what she'd agreed to, she reminded herself. She was lucky, even if she was filled with doubts right now. Mateo was a good man, a man she liked and trusted, even if love was never going to come into their particular equation. She had more, so much more, than most women of the world. She certainly wasn't going to complain.

But her heart felt as heavy as her dress as she prepared to make her official exit from the palace, and walk alone across the crowd-packed square to the cathedral where her groom—and a thousand guests—awaited.

As the doors were flung open, the bright sunlight streamed in, making Rachel squint. Francesca's hand was at her back, her voice a murmur in her ear.

'Chin up, eyes straight ahead. Nod, don't wave, in case you drop your bouquet.'

Rachel glanced down at the magnificent selection of white roses and lilies she'd been given for the photos. She gulped. 'Okay.'

'Walk slowly—right foot forward, feet together, and so on. It will feel a lot slower than you're used to. Count it in your head.'

'Okay,' Rachel said again. She wished they'd rehearsed this part, and not just what happened in the church, but it had sounded simple when the square was empty. All she had to do was walk across it.

'Go,' Francesca urged, and gave her a little push. Rachel stepped through the palace doors. The noise greeted her first, like a towering wave crashing over her. They were cheering. She, the nobody who had been overlooked by everyone for most of her life, even by her parents, now had what felt like the entire world screaming their approval. It was daunting, terrifying even, but also, surprisingly and amazingly, wonderful.

'Go,' Francesca whispered, and Rachel started down the shallow steps towards the square, her gown fanning behind her in an elegant arc of lace-edged satin. She knew she was meant to keep her gaze straight ahead, on the path that had been cleared through the crowd, with crowd barriers keeping everyone at bay, but she couldn't help but meet the gazes of some of the people who had queued for hours simply to be here, to see her.

'Queen Rachel!' someone called, and she nearly jerked in surprise. Queen Rachel. If that didn't sound crazily weird…

'You're so beautiful!' someone else shouted,

and she let her gaze move amidst the crowd, settling on as many faces as she could and offering them her smile. Her bouquet was too heavy for her to free one hand to wave, and she hoped her smile was enough.

'Thank you,' she heard herself saying. And then, *'Efharisto. Efharisto!'*

The cheers continued all the way across the square, which felt like a hundred miles instead of the equivalent in metres. On impulse, at the doors to the cathedral, she handed her bouquet to a waiting attendant and lifted her hand in a wave that sent the crowd cheering even more wildly. Then she reached for her bouquet and headed into the cool, hushed interior of the cathedral.

She blinked in the candle-flickering gloom, the brightly painted icons of saints visible high in the shadows of the huge cathedral. She took in the pews and pews filled with guests in their wedding finery, and there, at the start of a very long aisle, Mateo, standing by himself, looking devastating in a white tie and tails, bright red and blue royal regalia pinned to his chest. A king. *Her* king. Waiting to escort her down the aisle and to the ceremony.

For a second, poised on the threshold of her entire life, Rachel hesitated as a thousand thoughts tilted and slid through her mind. Her hands tightened on the bouquet as organ music crashed and swelled.

This was happening. She was doing this. *They* were doing this. And she hoped and prayed that somehow it would be the right thing for them both.

Mateo's gaze was fixed on his bride as she turned to face him. Her veil flowed over her shoulders in a lace river, her dress belling out behind in her in a floaty arc of satin. He reached out a hand and, with her gaze fixed on him, she took it. Her fingers slid across his and then tightened. The moment felt suspended, stretching on in significance, before Mateo turned and together they began to walk down the aisle.

He glanced at her as they walked—her chin tilted proudly, her shoulders back, her gaze straight ahead. She was elegant. Regal. Magnificent. Mateo's heart swelled with pride and something else, something dangerously deeper, as they walked towards the altar. All the unspoken tension and coolness that had existed between them for the last two days fell away in that moment. They were walking towards their future together, and she would soon be his.

The ceremony passed in a dazed blur. As was tradition, every vow was repeated three times, and wedding crowns of laurel placed on their heads, rings slipped onto their right hands, the hand of blessing. The music swelled and Mateo lifted her veil. She smiled at him tremulously, everything she felt and more in her eyes. He kissed her, barely a brush of her lips, but it felt like fireworks exploding in his head.

How was he going to stand this? How was he going to maintain that necessary distance for his own safety, as well as hers?

The questions fell into the tumult of his mind and were lost as the ceremony continued, into their coronation. Now husband and wife, they ascended the steps of the cathedral and knelt, hand in hand, before the two thrones there.

The bishop placed the historic crowns on their heads; the weight was surprising, and Mateo glanced at Rachel, a tremor rippling through him at the beautiful sight of her—wearing both a crown and a wedding dress. His bride. His Queen.

Then the ceremony was over, the crowns removed, and the music started again. After helping her to rise, Mateo escorted her back down the aisle. They were married. Husband and wife, for ever.

'Did that actually happen?' Rachel asked shakily as they stood on the steps of the cathedral, blinking in the bright sunlight.

'It most certainly did.' Mateo glanced down at the ring sparkling on his hand. He felt changed in a way he hadn't expected, on a molecular level. His whole *being* was changed, as if he'd undergone a chemical reaction without realising. He could never go back, and neither could Rachel.

'What do we do now?' Rachel asked. 'I know I've been told, but everything feels different now.'

'It does, doesn't it?' He felt a rush of gratitude and even joy that she felt the same as he did. They were *changed*.

'I mean, there's people, for one.' She gestured to the crowds who had been waiting for them to emerge. 'It's completely different, to walk across that square when it's filled with people.'

'Of course.' Mateo looked away, annoyed with himself for rushing to such a stupid, sentimental conclusion. They were changed. Right.

'So should we go? Or do we wait?'

'We can go.' His jaw tightened as he reached for her hand. 'Might as well get this over with.'

Hurt flashed in her eyes as she looked at him. 'Is that really how you see it, Mateo?' she asked quietly.

'I didn't mean anything by it,' he said a bit shortly, even though he had. He'd been reminding himself as well as her of what their marriage was really based on, and it wasn't some stupid rush of emotion.

'This is our wedding day,' Rachel stated with quiet dignity. 'The only one we'll ever have, God willing. Can't we enjoy it?'

He felt like a cad then, a real joy-stealing jerk.

'I'm sorry,' he said. 'Of course we can. Why don't we give them a kiss?'

'Wait—what?'

'A kiss,' he said more firmly, and took her into his arms. She came willingly, and as he settled his mouth on hers he felt a deep sense of satisfaction as well as a rush of desire. This part of their marriage, at least, didn't have to be so complicated.

Rachel's mouth opened like a flower under his and she reached up to cup his cheek with one hand, in an unsettlingly tender gesture. The crowd roared and stamped and whistled their approval. Reluctantly Mateo broke the kiss. His breathing was ragged and so was Rachel's.

'That's a deposit towards later,' he said, and she let out a little breathless laugh.

'Good to know.'

They started the traditional wedding walk across the square to the palace, where they would have a formal wedding breakfast, followed by the carriage ride and then later by a ball. People continued to cheer, reaching their hands across the barriers. It was usual royal protocol to ignore such gestures, but Rachel broke ranks and starting shaking people's hands, and Mateo started to restrain her before he saw how people were responding to her—with both devotion and joy.

Mateo had always intended to model his kingship on his father's, to be dignified, a bit austere and remote, but also sincere and hardworking. His father would never have shaken a commoner's hand, never mind posing for a selfie as Rachel was now doing. And yet when Mateo saw the reaction of his people, their unfettered delight, he realised that this might be what was needed.

His father had kept the public at a distance, thinking he was above them, and Leo had ignored them in pursuit of his own private pleasure. Maybe it was time for Mateo to be different. For the King and Queen to engage with their people, to love them as their own.

The thought was novel, a bit alarming, and yet also strangely exciting.

'They love you,' Mateo murmured as they finally cleared the crowds and entered the palace. 'They really love you.'

'It's so strange,' she murmured, shaking her head, looking dazed. 'I've never…' She stopped, but something in her tone made Mateo turn to her.

'You never what?'

She paused, biting her lip as she gazed at him uncertainly. 'I've never been loved before,' she confessed with a shaky laugh. 'By anyone. But I think I could get used to it.'

It was such a dramatic statement that Mateo shook his head instinctively. 'Of course you've been loved.'

'No, not really.'

'Your mother. Your parents—'

'No. Not like that, anyway.'

He frowned, searching her face, looking for self-pity but finding only her usual good-humoured pragmatism. 'What are you talking about, Rachel?'

'My parents didn't love me,' she said simply. 'Or at least, they didn't like me. Which is worse, do you think?' She posed it like an academic question.

'Of course your parents loved you.' Even though he'd rebelled as a youth, even though he'd resented being seen as unnecessary in the line to the throne, and walked away from everything as a result, he'd never doubted his parents' love. *Never.* Yet Rachel spoke about her loveless parents as if she was simply stating facts.

'I suppose they loved me after a fashion,' she said after a moment. 'I mean, they provided for me, certainly. But they didn't act as if they loved me, or wanted me in their lives, so I didn't feel loved.' She shrugged. 'But why on earth are we talking about this now? We need to go into the wedding breakfast.'

'They must have loved you.' Mateo didn't know why he was labouring the point, only that he really hated the idea that Rachel had grown up unloved. Disliked, even. *Rachel.* 'Maybe they were just reticent...'

She rolled her eyes. 'Okay. Sure. That's what they were. Can we go now?'

It was obvious she wanted to drop it, and now was hardly the time or place for some sort of emotional discussion—the kind of discussion he'd never really wanted to have—and yet Mateo was realising what a fool he'd been, to think he could separate parts of his life—his heart—like oil and water, never mixing. Marriage wasn't like that. It was a chemical reaction, just as he'd felt in himself; two separate entities combining and becoming something new. Hydrogen and oxygen turning into life-giving water. Or perhaps caesium and water, causing a life-threatening explosion. *Which was it?*

Only time would tell. And whichever it was, Mateo knew he couldn't take the affection and the trust and the physical desire and compartmentalise them all, neatly labelled, put away in a drawer and never causing him any bother. As much as he wanted to, needed to, he couldn't.

And that was when Mateo knew he was in big trouble.

CHAPTER THIRTEEN

RACHEL'S HEART FLUTTERED like a wild thing in her chest as Mateo closed the door of the bedroom. They were in the honeymoon suite, tucked away in a tower in a far wing of the palace, with a view of the sea shimmering under the moonlight from its high windows.

The circular room was something out of another fairy tale—*Rapunzel*, perhaps—with a twisting staircase that led up to this lovely room, a cosy fire crackling in the grate, and a canopied king-sized bed draped in silks and satins of various shades of ivory and taupe taking pride of place.

Rachel released a shuddery breath she hadn't even realised she'd been holding. It had been a long day, an endless day, from the ceremony and coronation this morning to the formal wedding breakfast with speeches and toasts, posing for photo after photo, and then the carriage ride around the old city, and finally a ball to finish.

She'd changed into another gown, the one she wore now, a strapless ball gown in taupe satin and a diamanté-encrusted band around her waist.

At least she and Mateo hadn't had to dance in front of everyone, although after three glasses of champagne she'd managed a simple swaying with him to a modern pop song. Mateo had smiled down at her as they had danced, but she hadn't been able to gauge his mood, just as she hadn't been able to all day. Just as she couldn't now.

He turned from the door, his expression inscrutable as he loosened his white tie. Rachel watched him, feeling like a mouse being observed by a hawk, although there was nothing particularly predatory about his cool blue-green gaze. She was just feeling uncertain and vulnerable now that they'd finally reached this moment, the moment when they were alone together. When they would truly become husband and wife.

'It's very late,' Mateo remarked. 'We don't have to do anything tonight.'

Rachel couldn't keep disappointment from swooping inside her. Clearly he wasn't in any rush.

'We might as well get it over with,' she tossed back at him, echoing his words from this morning that had hurt her more than they should have.

'Is that how you view it?' His lips twisted and he tossed his tie aside.

'It's not how I want to view it,' she returned. The last thing she wanted to do was argue *now*. 'I'm not trying to sound snippy, but I have no idea how you feel about this, Mateo.'

'This?'

'Us.' She gestured to the bed. 'You *know*.'

'Sex?' he stated baldly, and for some reason she flinched. He made it sound like some sort of physical procedure they had to perform, rather than the joyful consummation of their marriage.

'Yes,' she muttered, and suddenly found herself fighting tears. She turned away from him, not wanting him to see, but he caught her arm.

'Rachel.'

'What...?' she managed thickly, blinking as fast as she could to keep the tears back. A few fell anyway.

'I'm sorry. I think I'm being an ass.'

'You think?'

'All right. I am. I'm sorry. I don't...' He blew out a breath. 'This is strange for me too.'

'Not as strange as it is for me,' she returned tartly, and he frowned at her.

'What do you mean?'

'I have a feeling that my experience is significantly more limited than yours,' she informed him, knowing it needed to be said even as she wished that it didn't.

'Oh?' Mateo gazed at her appraisingly. 'You might be wrong.'

She almost laughed at that. 'I don't think so.'

'I'm not some Lothario, Rachel. Work has been my mistress more than any woman.' His mouth curved in a crooked smile. 'I've spent far more time with you than anyone else, you know.'

'As gratified as I am to hear that, I still stand by my statement.' She felt her cheeks heat as she confessed, 'I have *very* little experience, Mateo.'

His narrowed gaze scanned her face. 'You're… you're not a virgin,' he stated, not quite making it a question.

'No…but almost.'

'How can you be almost?'

She pressed her hands to her cheeks, willing her blush to fade. 'This is seriously embarrassing, you know?'

'You don't have to be embarrassed with me.' He made it sound so obvious, but it wasn't.

'I do, especially when you turn all brooding and remote on me, and make me feel as if I don't know you at all.'

'Brooding and remote?' The corner of his mouth lifted in a smile. 'Just slap me when I do that.'

'I might.'

'Seriously, Rachel.' He took a step towards her, his shirt open at the throat, his gaze a bit hooded, his eyes so bright and his hair so dark and his jaw so hard… He was just too beautiful. It should have been a crime. It certainly wasn't fair. 'Tell me.'

'Tell you what? How little experience I have when it comes to this?' She gestured to the bed.

'Only if it would make you feel better, to have me know.'

'One time, okay?' The words rang out and she closed her eyes in mortification. 'I've done it one time, and, trust me, it was completely forgettable.' There. It was out. Thirty-two years old and she'd had sex *once*, with a guy who had turned out to be a complete cad. But she didn't want to go into those humiliating details now.

'Okay,' Mateo said after a moment.

'Okay?' Rachel stared at him uncertainly.

'Now I know.' Mateo shrugged. 'It doesn't make any difference to me. I'm not put off, if that's what you're afraid of.'

'Not *yet*.'

'Not ever. A lack of experience isn't a turn-off, Rachel, trust me.'

'That's assuming you're turned *on* in the first place,' she muttered. She felt tears again, and tried to hide it. This was all getting a bit too much.

'Why would you think I wouldn't be?'

'Why would I think you would?' she challenged. 'We've known each other for ten years, Mateo, and you haven't felt anything like that for me in all that time.'

'And nor have you for me,' Mateo countered. Rachel decided to remain silent on that point. There was only so much honesty she could take. 'It's changed now. We're looking at each other differently now.'

'You haven't exactly had trouble keeping your hands off me,' she felt compelled to point out. 'Quite the opposite. We've kissed exactly three times since we've been engaged.'

Mateo's lids lowered as he looked at her meaningfully. 'We've done more than kiss.'

'Barely. And even then you were pretty quick to haul me off your lap.' The humiliation of that moment stung all over again, and a tear fell. She dashed it away hurriedly and Mateo swore under his breath.

'Rachel, I had no idea you felt this way.' He looked flummoxed; the colour leached from his face as he shook his head slowly.

'I'm not expecting you to fall in love with me,' she managed stiltedly. 'Or even be wild with passion for me. I know I'm not exactly—'

'*Don't* say it.' Mateo sounded fierce. 'Don't run yourself down, Rachel. You're amazing. You're beautiful. You're my *wife*.'

'Then show me,' she whispered brokenly. *'Show me.'*

Mateo held her gaze for one blazing second and then he swiftly crossed the room and, cupping her face in his hands, kissed her deeply.

He'd kissed her before, and it had always made her senses spin. Now was no different, as his mouth slanted and then settled over hers and his tongue swept the softness inside, making her body sag and her knees weaken. He kissed her as if he *knew* her. And that made all the difference.

Rachel wrapped her arms around his hard body and he pressed closer, one knee sliding between the billowing folds of her gown as his kiss took possession of her, and her spinning senses started to drown. She was overwhelmed. Overloaded. Undone. And all by one kiss.

When he finally lifted his head to give her a questioning, demanding look, she managed the weakest smile she'd ever given.

'That's a start.'

'A *start*?' he growled, and he kissed her again. Deeper this time, until she was truly and utterly lost, and yet at the same time found. She'd never been kissed like this before. She'd never felt like this before. And she wanted more.

Mateo broke the kiss to give her another one of his burning looks. Then he began to unbutton his shirt. Rachel swallowed hard.

'I've never seen you without your shirt on before,' she remarked conversationally, except her voice came out in a croak.

'You're going to see me with a whole lot less on than that.'

Rachel gulped—and then thought of her wobbly bits that she wasn't sure she wanted Mateo seeing. 'Maybe we should move to the bed,' she suggested. 'Get under the covers.'

Mateo arched an eyebrow. 'Are you trying to hide from me?'

'A little,' she confessed. 'Let's face it, Mateo, when it comes to basic good looks—'

He laid a finger against her lips. 'I don't want to hear it. Not one more disparaging word. This is our wedding night, Rachel, and you are a beautiful, gorgeous, sexy *queen*. Don't ever forget it.'

His finger was still against her lips as she regarded him with wide eyes. 'I won't,' she whispered, and then Mateo lifted his finger from her lips and finished unbuttoning his shirt, shrugging it off his broad shoulders in one sinuous movement.

He was breathtakingly beautiful, all hard, sculpted muscles, pecs and abs burnished and defined, making Rachel long to touch him, but she felt too timid.

Mateo met her shyly questioning gaze. 'Touch me,' he commanded, and so she did.

The trail of Rachel's fingertips along his abdomen had Mateo's muscles flexing involuntarily. Her hesitant caress was positively enflaming, with an intensity he hadn't expected. He *responded* to this woman, and it wasn't just merely physical. Her artless confession, her shy looks, that small smile, *everything…*

It humbled him, that Rachel was so honest. She'd experienced so little in life—so little love, so little desire—and yet she'd still held onto her pragmatic attitude, her good humour. And even though the intensity of his own feeling, as well as the intimacy of Rachel's confession, had Mateo instinctively wanting to throw up all the old barricades, he didn't.

Because this wasn't about him, or at least not just him. It was about Rachel, and showing her how beautiful and desirable she was. It was about making her feel cherished and wanted, because right now Mateo realised he wanted that for her more than anything. More than his instinct for self-protection. He could give her this. He *needed* to give her this.

Her fingers skimmed up his chest and she looked at him with a question in her eyes. 'You can touch me a lot more than that,' he told her. 'But first we need to get some clothes off.'

Her eyes widened and she bit her lip. She was nervous about being naked in front of him. Mateo knew that, and it felt like a gift. He would cherish it. Cherish her.

'Turn around,' he said softly, and slowly she did.

Her ball gown had about a thousand tiny buttons from the middle of her back right down to the base. Mateo began undoing them one by one as Rachel sucked in a hard breath.

'I think there's a lovely nightgown around here somewhere,' she said shakily. 'Francesca picked it out…'

'We'll save it for later.' His fingers skimmed her skin as he slid each button from its hole, revealing the smooth, silky expanse of her back. He spread his hands, enjoying the whisper-soft feel of her skin against his palms. With the last button undone, the dress fell about her waist. The gown had had a built-in bra, and so there was nothing on her top half and Mateo liked it that way.

He reached around and filled his hands with the warm softness of her breasts, and she let out a shocked gasp at his touch. After a second she leaned back against him and he brushed his thumbs across her nipples, making them both shudder. Her gown slithered lower on her hips, and it only took one swift tug to have it falling in a crumpled heap around her calves.

Taking a deep breath, Rachel stepped out of it, and then turned to face him, her heart—and all her fear—in her eyes. She wore nothing but a lacy slip of underwear, and a pair of stockings with lace garters. Her hair had half fallen out of the elegant up-do, and lay in tumbled, chestnut waves over her shoulders. Her cheeks were flushed, her lips bee-stung, her eyes like stars. And her *body*...all the blood rushed from his head as Mateo gazed upon her.

'Rachel,' he said in a voice that throbbed both with sincerity and desire. 'You are truly beautiful.'

'I feel beautiful,' she whispered, sounding amazed, and Mateo reached for her. The press of her breasts against his bare chest was exquisite, but he wanted more. He let her go to briefly shrug out of his clothes, muttering with impatience as he fumbled with his waistcoat, the faff of his trouser buttons. Finally he was free, as nearly naked as she was, and he drew her to the bed.

They fell upon it in a tangle of covers and limbs, and Mateo ran one hand from her ankle to her hip, revelling in the silken sweetness of her skin.

'Touch me, too,' he whispered and she pressed her palm flat against his chest, before an impish smile came over her face and she trailed her hand down and down, wrapping her fingers around the throbbing heat of him.

'I've never done this before,' she whispered

as her fingers explored and stroked. 'Am I doing it right?'

Mateo could not keep from groaning aloud. 'Yes,' he told her as she continued her artless, and very effective, caresses. *'Yes.'*

She continued to stroke and explore, her caresses becoming less and less hesitant, making his blood heat and his mind blur. He was going to lose his self-control very, very soon.

'This might surprise you,' he managed as he gently but firmly removed her hand, 'but I am not nearly as experienced as you seem to think I am, and it has been rather a long time since I have been in this type of situation.'

Her eyes widened as she looked at him. 'Really?'

'Really. And if you keep doing what you're doing, our wedding night will be rather short and, I fear, even more disappointing. So let me touch you now.'

A small smile curved her mouth as he gently pushed her onto her back. 'All right.'

Mateo kissed her on her mouth, savouring the sweetness of her lips, before he moved lower, kissing his way from her jaw to her throat, and then taking his time to lavish each of her lovely breasts with his full attention. The mewling sounds she made enflamed him further, and he moved lower, his tongue skimming the gently rounded beauty of her belly to settle happily between her thighs.

'Mateo...' Her fingers threaded through his hair as her hips lifted instinctively and Mateo tasted his fill.

Rachel's cry shattered the air as her body shuddered with her first climax. Mateo intended there to be several.

'Oh, my goodness…' she managed faintly, and Mateo smiled against her skin. 'I've never…'

'Now you have.'

She laughed at that and he rolled on top of her, bracing himself on his forearms, as he looked down at her, flushed and sated, yet clearly ready for more. 'Oh…' she breathed as he nudged at her entrance. She wriggled underneath him, a look of concentration on her face as she angled herself upwards, ever the scientist looking for the perfect conditions for an experiment.

And the conditions were perfect, Mateo acknowledged as he slid slowly, inch by exquisite inch, inside her. Rachel's eyes widened and her lips parted and she hooked one leg around his waist to draw him even deeper, so their bodies felt totally enmeshed, utterly entwined. *As one.*

Here was the ultimate chemical reaction, where something new was created from two separate substances, and could never, ever be torn apart.

Mateo began to move, and Rachel moved with

him, hesitant at first but then with sinuous certainty, and they found their rhythm together as easily as if they'd always known it, minds and bodies and hearts all melded.

It was wonderfully strange and yet as natural as breathing, as they climbed higher and higher towards the pleasure that was promised both of them, just out of reach until it burst upon them like a dazzling firework, and then, with a gasp and a cry, they fell apart, reassembling themselves together, as one, their bodies still entwined, their arms around each other as their releases shuddered through them.

Mateo rolled onto his back, taking Rachel with him, their hearts thudding against one another with frantic beats.

He'd meant to offer this—himself—as a gift to her, but it wasn't, he realised now, that simple an exchange. He couldn't give without receiving. He couldn't offer himself and at the same time keep himself separate.

If he'd thought he was in trouble this morning, after the ceremony, he knew he was utterly lost now. Lost—and yet found. And the thought terrified him, not for his own safety or self-protection, but for Rachel's.

He could not hold her heart in his hands. He could not bear to, for he would surely, surely shatter it.

CHAPTER FOURTEEN

'THANK YOU SO much for your contribution, Your Highness.'

Rachel smiled and nodded graciously at the head teacher of the girls' high school in Constanza, where she'd been part of a round-table discussion on encouraging female pupils to study STEM subjects. The conversation had been wide-ranging and invigorating, and she'd enjoyed every minute of it.

'Thank you for inviting me,' she said as she took her leave, pausing for a photo op before shaking hands with everyone at the table. A few minutes later she was in the back of a black SUV, speeding back towards the palace.

It had been a month since her wedding, and Rachel had done her best to fully involve herself as Queen. She'd selected several charities to support, and said yes to almost every engagement at which she'd been asked to appear. Maybe if she kept herself busy enough, she wouldn't notice the empty space in her heart.

She had nothing to complain about, Rachel reminded herself severely. It was a talking-to she had to give herself almost every day. Absolutely nothing to complain about, because she'd agreed to this; she'd known what she was getting into; she'd accepted the deal with full understanding of what it had meant.

She just hadn't realised how it would *feel.*

Since their wonderful and frankly earth-shattering wedding night, Rachel had had hopes that something more—something a lot like love—would blossom between them, in time. When Mateo had held her to him, moved inside her, buried his face in her hair…

She'd been so sure. Everything had felt possible.

But in the month since that night, that incandescent sense of possibility had begun to fade, day by day and night by night. Mateo wasn't cruel, or cold, or even cool. He was exactly what he'd said he'd be—a trusted friend, an affectionate partner. But he didn't love her, Rachel knew that full well, and while she'd agreed in theory to a marriage based on friendship rather than love, she'd assumed it would mean that neither of them loved the other.

Not, Rachel acknowledged hollowly as she

watched the streets of Constanza slide by, that she would fall in love with a man who was determined not to love her. Who kept part of his heart clearly roped off, who had a shadow in his eyes and a certain distance in his demeanour that even a passionate night of lovemaking—not that she could even call it lovemaking—could banish.

And meanwhile she felt herself tumbling headlong into something she was afraid was love. The kind of soul-deep, long-abiding love she had never expected to feel for anyone. But Mateo had been so kind...had made her feel so valued... had held her like a treasure and laughed with her and given her joy. Of course she'd fallen in love with him.

It was just he hadn't fallen in love with her, and had no intention of ever doing so, as far as Rachel could see.

The SUV drove through the palace gates and then up to the front doors. A footman hurried out to open Rachel's door, bowing as she stepped out. Four weeks of this kind of treatment and it still felt surreal. Rachel thanked him and then walked into the palace, heading for her private suite of rooms. It still felt strange, to live in a palace rather than her own home.

Although Mateo had assured her she could redecorate her suite as she liked, Rachel hadn't dared touch any of the antiques or oil paintings, the silk hangings and fine furnishings. As a result she felt as if she lived in a five-star hotel rather than a home, which was sometimes nice and sometimes a bit disconcerting.

'Your Highness, you're back.'

Rachel turned to give her personal assistant a smile. 'Yes, I am.'

'The discussion was productive?'

'Very much so, I believe. Do I have anything scheduled for the rest of the day, Monica?'

'I don't believe there is anything on your schedule until a dinner tomorrow night.'

'Right.' Rachel paused as she took off the heels she still hadn't got used to wearing. 'And do you happen to know where the King is?' she asked casually.

Monica's face was carefully blank. 'I believe he is out.'

'Thank you.' She dismissed her assistant with a smile and a small wave.

Alone in her suite Rachel drifted around, grateful for an unscheduled afternoon and yet still feeling a bit lost. She'd seen very little of Mateo in the last month, besides formal events and nights—nights which were seared on her mind and made her body tingle. Still, she missed spending time with him, missed the easy friendship they'd once had, when it hadn't been complicated by the demands of royalty—and marriage.

Even if he would never love her, she wished he'd spend time with her.

She had just changed into comfortable clothes and settled on a sofa by the window with her laptop, hoping to catch up on some emails to friends, when a light knock sounded on her door.

'Yes?'

'Hello.' Mateo popped his head around the door, giving her a wry smile. 'Are you busy?'

'Busy? No.' Rachel closed her laptop, trying to temper the feeling of delight that was spreading through her like warm, golden honey. Perhaps he just had a quick question to ask, and then he'd be on his way…

'I thought we could spend the afternoon together,' Mateo said, an unusual note of hesitation in his voice. 'If you wanted to.'

If? The smile that bloomed across Rachel's face was impossible to suppress, not that she even wanted to. 'I'd love that.'

'Good.'

'What did you have in mind?'

'I thought we could go sailing, just the two of us.'

'On our own?' After being shadowed by security and staff for the last month, the prospect was wonderfully liberating.

'We'll leave the security on the shore. They can't live in my pocket all the time.'

Rachel frowned. 'Are you sure it will be safe?'

'No one's knows where we're going.' Mateo shrugged. 'It would be good to get away.'

Yes, it would. And the fact that Mateo wanted to spend time alone with her was intoxicating. 'All right,' Rachel said. 'When do you want to go?'

'How long until you're ready?'

She laughed. 'Five minutes.'

And it was only five minutes later that they were driving in a dark green convertible, a palace car Rachel hadn't seen before, but much preferred to the heavy SUVS with their blacked-out windows.

With the sky bright blue above them and the sea sparkling below, the day felt full of promise.

'Where are we going, exactly?' Rachel asked.

'A private marina where there's a sailboat.'

'I didn't even know you could sail,' she said with a laugh. Mateo threw her a glinting smile.

'There's a lot of things you don't know about me.'

Today, with the sun shining and the sky so blue, that felt like a promise rather than a warning. Rachel smiled back.

Half an hour later they were on a small sailing raft heading out into the shimmering blue-green waters of the Mediterranean Sea, with not a security officer or staff member in sight.

'Where are we going now?' Rachel asked as she tilted her face to the sun. 'Do you have a destination?'

'As a matter of fact, I do. There is a small island out here—not much more than a speck of land, but it has a nice beach. I used to go here when I was younger.'

'To get away from it all?' Rachel teased, and Mateo gave a grimacing nod.

'Actually, yes. When I was out here, I could forget I was a prince.'

'Was that something you wanted to forget?' Rachel asked softly. She was aware, not for the first time, of all she didn't know. She didn't know about Mateo's family, really, only that he was the youngest of three brothers. One had died, and one had walked away. Both, she realised now, must have left scars.

'Sometimes it was,' Mateo answered after a moment, his narrowed gaze on the glinting sea. 'I'd always get punished for trying to escape. Sent to my room with no dinner. I suppose I deserved it.'

'Your parents must have been worried about you.'

'I suppose.'

'You don't sound convinced.'

He shrugged. 'As the third son, and a later surprise at that, I was a bit of an afterthought.'

Rachel frowned. 'Were you neglected?'

'No, not at all. In some ways, it was a blessing—I had so much more freedom than either Kosmos or Leo.'

'Tell me about your brothers,' she said. 'I've never heard you speak of them before.'

'I suppose I haven't had much to say.' He nodded towards the sea ahead of them, and the shape of an island now visible. 'Let me get us to the shore.'

They spent the next few moments navigating the waters, and then mooring the boat in an inlet of a postage-stamp-sized island, no more than a strip of beach and a bit of scrub. With the sea stretching in every direction, Rachel couldn't imagine a lonelier or lovelier spot.

'I brought a picnic,' Mateo told her as he reached for a wicker basket. 'Or rather, I had the kitchen make one for me.'

'Isn't that how kings always do things?' Rachel teased as she took his hand and he helped her out of the boat. She couldn't remember when they'd last talked so much, or when she'd felt so happy. This was what she'd imagined, what she'd longed for—their friendship back, but something more as well.

They strolled hand in hand onto the beach, and Mateo spread out a blanket before opening the picnic basket and setting out a variety of tempting goodies—strawberries, smoked salmon, crusty bread, a ripe cheese, and, of course, champagne.

It was perfect, Rachel thought as he popped the cork on the bottle and poured them both glasses.

Everything was perfect.

Mateo hadn't planned any of this. It was strange, but his own actions were taking him by surprise. It felt as if one moment he'd been sitting in his study, staring out at the blue sky, and the next he'd jumped into a boat and sailed for the blue yonder.

Not that he regretted what he'd done. In fact, he couldn't remember the last time he'd felt so relaxed, so free. He took a sip of champagne and closed his eyes, enjoying the sunlight on his face.

He realised he didn't even mind talking to Rachel about things he tried never to think about, never mind discuss—his family, his brothers, the deep-seated desire he'd had not to be a prince—or even a king. Yet somehow it felt different out here, sipping champagne on the sand, the barriers gone or at least a little lowered, the whole world wide open.

'When did your older brother die?' Rachel asked quietly, her generous mouth curved downwards, her eyes as soft as a bed of pansies.

'Ten years ago. A sailing accident.'

'Sailing…' Those soft eyes widened and she

glanced instinctively at the little boat bobbing gently on the waves.

'Kosmos was a risk-taker. He loved living dangerously. He took a boat out during dangerous conditions, and sailed through a storm.' Mateo remembered the shock of hearing the news, the sudden fury that his older brother, more of a distant, admired figure than someone he'd felt truly close to, could be so careless.

'That was right when we started working together.' Rachel frowned. 'You never told me.'

'We barely knew each other then.'

'It's more than that, Mateo.' She paused, seeming to weigh her words. 'Why did you never confide in me? I don't mean about the royalty thing, which I actually do understand keeping to yourself. But other things. Your brother's death. Your father's death.'

Mateo considered the question for a moment, rather than dismiss it out of hand, as he normally would have, saying, *I never talk about myself.* Or, *There was never a good time.*

'I don't know,' he said at last. 'I suppose because, in doing so, I would have revealed something about myself.' As soon as he said the words, he felt weirdly vulnerable, and yet also relieved.

Rachel kept her soft gaze steady on him. 'Something you didn't want others to see?'

He shrugged. 'I was never that close to Kosmos

or Leo. I looked up to them, but they were both older than me and they were very close themselves. They had a similar set of experiences—the heir and spare preparing for a life in the royal spotlight, while I was left to do more or less as I pleased.'

'That sounds lonely.'

'Like I said before, it had its benefits.'

'Even so.' Her quietly compassionate tone was nearly the undoing of him. Emotions he hadn't even realised he'd been holding onto, buried deep, started to bubble up. Mateo took a sip of champagne in an effort to keep it all at bay. 'It must have been a shock, when you were told you had to be King.'

'It was,' he agreed. He thought his voice was neutral but something must have given him away because Rachel leaned forward and laid her hand over his.

'You're doing an amazing job, Mateo. *You're* amazing. I know I don't even know a tenth of what you do, and with the talk of insurgency and this economic thing…' She laughed softly. 'I don't know much about it, but I know you are doing the best job you can, giving two hundred per cent all the time.'

'As a scientist, you should know better than to use the erroneous phrase two hundred per cent,' he quipped, because to take her seriously would be to very nearly weep.

'I'm a scientist, not a mathematician,' she retorted with a smile. 'And I'm not taking back any of it.'

He shook his head, smiling to cover how much her words meant, how thankful he was for her. He wanted to tell her as much, but he couldn't manage it because he felt too much and he wasn't used to it.

For fifteen years he'd kept himself from deep relationships, from love, because he was afraid of being hurt the way he'd been before, but more importantly, more deeply, because he was afraid of hurting another person. He couldn't live with that kind of guilt and grief again, and yet here he was, treading on the thinnest of ice, in telling Rachel these things. In starting to care, and letting her care about him.

He should stop it right now, but the truth was he didn't want to. It felt too much, but part of that was good. It was wonderful.

'I know you don't want to hear anything soppy,' she continued with an uncertain smile, 'but I'm going to tell you anyway.'

'I consider myself warned,' he said lightly, although his heart gave an unpleasant little lurch. Was she going to tell him she loved him? He would not know how to handle that.

'You've given me such confidence, Mateo,' Rachel said quietly. 'I haven't told you much about Josh except that he didn't break my heart. And he really didn't. But he broke my confidence—not that I had that much to begin with.'

'How…?' Mateo asked, although from what Rachel had already told him, he thought he could guess. She sighed.

'He was older than me, worldly and sophisticated. I had a crush on him. I suppose it was obvious.'

'So what happened, exactly?' Mateo asked, although judging by Rachel's tone, the look of resignation and remembrance in her eyes, he wasn't sure he wanted to know.

'I suppose if it had been a romance novel, I would have said he seduced me. But if it was a romance, he wasn't the hero.'

'The one time?' Mateo surmised.

She nodded. 'And the worst part was, afterwards he acted as if he didn't know me. I bounced into class the next day, full of hope, of certainty. I thought we were a couple. He acted as if he couldn't remember my name. Literally.' She tried to laugh but didn't quite manage it. 'And then I overheard him joking to his friends, about how it would have to be a really desperate guy who was willing to…you know…with me.'

'Oh, Rachel.' Mateo couldn't get any other

words out. He hated the bastard Josh for what he'd done—the careless, callous disregard he'd shown for someone as lovely and genuine and pure as Rachel.

'Anyway, I was telling you all this not to throw myself a pity party, but because you've changed that, Mateo. You've changed *me*. I used to always feel about myself—my body, my looks—the way he did. As if I was beneath notice. Easily forgettable. But when you look at me…' Her voice trailed off and blush pinked her cheeks as she tremulously met his gaze. 'I feel different. I feel…desirable. For the first time in my life. And that's been wonderful.' She gave an uncertain little laugh and Mateo did the only thing he could do, the only thing he wanted to do. He leaned forward and kissed her.

Her lips were soft and tasted of champagne and she let out a breathy sigh as he deepened the kiss. She grabbed his shoulder to steady herself but even so they ended up sprawled on the sand, the kiss going on and on and on.

He slipped his hand under her T-shirt and revelled in the warm softness of her body. As he tugged on her capri bottoms she let out a little laugh.

'Here…?'

'Why not? It's not as if anyone can see.' He smiled down at her and she blinked up at him, a look of wonder in her eyes. She cupped his face with her hands and for a second Mateo's heart felt like a cracked vessel that had been filled to the brim—overflowing and leaking, going everywhere. She'd done this to him. She'd awakened the heart he'd thought had been frozen for ever behind a paralysing wall of grief and fear. Love was too dangerous to consider, and yet here he was. Here *they* were.

'Rachel…' He couldn't bring himself to say the words, but he *felt* them, and he thought she saw it in his eyes as she brought his face down to hers and kissed him with both sweet innocence and passionate fervour. With everything she had. And Mateo responded in kind, moulding his body to hers, wanting only to keep this moment between them for ever.

CHAPTER FIFTEEN

RACHEL WAS HAPPY. It was a frail, fragile thing, like gossamer thread or a rose just about to bloom—all it would take was a gentle breeze to blow it all away. But, still, she was happy.

Since their afternoon on the island, Rachel had sensed a shift in Mateo, a softening. He'd willingly talked about his family, his emotions—things that Rachel had sensed had been off-limits before. The aloofness she'd felt from him since their marriage—the shadow lurking in his eyes, the slight repressiveness of his tone—had gone. Mostly.

Mateo, Rachel suspected, was a man at war with himself. He was starting to fall in love with her—if only she really could believe that!—but he didn't want to. At least, that was her take on the matter, and Agathe surprised her by agreeing.

They'd been having lunch in one of the palace's many salons when Agathe had said quite out of the blue, 'You must be patient with him, my dear.'

Rachel had nearly choked on a scallop. 'Pardon?'

'Mateo. I know he can be…difficult. Remote. It's his way of coping.'

Rachel absorbed that remark, tried not to let it hurt. 'What is he coping with?' she asked even as she thought, *Me?* Was his marriage something her husband had to *cope* with?

'Everything,' Agathe answered with a sad little sigh. 'The pressures of the kingship, certainly. His father was the same.'

'Was he?' Once again Rachel realised how little she knew about the Karavitis family.

'My husband believed he needed to keep a certain distance between him and his people. It was a matter of respect and authority. I don't know if he was right or not, but Mateo feels the responsibility, especially when he was never meant to have any royal role at all. I am afraid we did not prepare him as we should have.'

'Yet he is rising to the challenge,' Rachel returned, a fierce note of pride in her voice.

'Indeed he is, but at what cost?' Agathe smiled sadly. 'But it is more than that. Mateo has lost so many people…if he closes himself off, it's because he doesn't want to risk losing anyone else. Losing you. But it doesn't mean he doesn't love you.'

'You don't know that,' Rachel said after a

moment. She paused, deliberating whether she should mention the person who was still utterly off-limits. 'Sometimes I wonder if he has any more room to love, after…' she took a quick breath '…after Cressida.'

Agathe's face softened into sympathetic lines. 'Of course he does. His relationship to Cressida… that was no more than schoolboy infatuation.'

'He doesn't talk about it like that,' Rachel said, even though she desperately wanted to believe it. 'He won't talk about it at all.' Agathe nodded slowly, and Rachel looked down at her plate. 'I shouldn't be talking to you about this. I know Mateo wouldn't like it.' He'd feel as if she'd betrayed him, and she couldn't stand that thought.

'Give him time,' Agathe said by way of answer. 'Be patient…and believe.'

Rachel was still holding onto those words, praying they were a promise, when she got ready for an engagement in Constanza one foggy afternoon in November. She and Mateo had been married for six weeks, and winter had finally hit the island country, with thick, rolling fog and damp, freezing temperatures.

Mateo remained as busy as ever, but not as aloof, and Rachel continued to feel she had reason to hope. To believe. And, she reminded herself, she was happy.

A knock on her bedroom door had her turning,

expecting Monica to tell her the car was ready to take her into the city. To her surprise, Mateo stood there, stealing her breath as he always did, wearing a navy-blue suit with a dark green tie that brought out the brightness of his eyes.

'You have an engagement?' he asked and she nodded as she fastened the second of her pearl earrings. 'Yes, at the bazaar in the city. Supporting women stallholders.'

'In the bazaar?' Mateo frowned. 'That's not the safest place.'

'I'll have my usual security.' Rachel glanced at him in concern. 'Has something happened? Are you worried?'

'No, I just don't like you being in such an exposed, rough place.'

'It's a market, not a Mafia den,' Rachel told him with a little laugh. 'I'm sure I'll be fine.'

Mateo nodded slowly, still looking less than pleased. 'I suppose so.'

He didn't sound convinced and Rachel laid a hand on his arm. 'Is there something you're not telling me, Mateo?'

He hesitated, his lowered gaze on her hand still resting on his arm. 'The insurgents are still active,' he admitted after a moment.

'But in the north…'

'Yes, but it isn't that far away.'

Nerves fluttered in Rachel's stomach at his

grim tone. 'Surely they're not in the bazaar?' she asked, trying for a light tone and almost managing it.

Mateo was silent for a long moment, his gaze still lowered. 'No,' he said at last. 'Of course not.'

'Then I'll be fine.' She looked at him directly, willing him to meet her gaze. When he did, the look on his face—a mixture of resolution and despair—made her want to put her arms around him. Tell him she wouldn't go.

But then his lips curved in a quick smile and he nodded. 'It will be fine, I'm sure. I'll see you later today, for dinner.'

'All right.' He gave her a quick kiss on the cheek and as Rachel watched him walk away she had a strange, tumbling sensation that she forced herself to banish. Mateo's worries were just that—worries. Worries of a king who cared too much, who had lost people before. She was just going to the city's bazaar; she'd be surrounded by security. And really, she should be pleased that Mateo cared so much. Another sign, she wondered, that he was coming to love her? Or just wishful thinking?

An hour later Rachel had banished all her concerns as well as Mateo's as she entered the colourful bazaar with its rickety stalls and colourful banners. She spent an enjoyable hour meeting with the female stallholders and chatting about the goods they sold—handmade batik cloth; small honey cakes dotted with sesame seeds; hand-tooled leather wallets and purses.

She was impressed by their ingenuity and determination, and charmed by their ready smiles and cheerful demeanour. They faced far more challenges than she ever had, and yet they'd kept their heads as well as their smiles.

She was just saying goodbye when she felt the heavy hand of one of her security guards, Matthias, on her shoulder.

'Your Royal Highness, we need to go.'

'We're not in a rush—' Rachel began, only to have Matthias grip her elbow firmly and start to hustle her through the crowds and alleyways of the bazaar.

'There is a disturbance.'

'A disturbance—?' Rachel began, craning her neck to see what he meant.

In her six weeks as a royal, she'd become used to being guarded, even as she'd believed it to be unnecessary. There had never been any 'disturbances', and the unrest Mateo spoke of in the north was nothing more than a vague idea.

Now, as she saw Matthias with one hand on her elbow, one hand on the pistol at his hip, she felt a flicker of the kind of fear she'd never experienced before.

This couldn't be happening. This couldn't be

real. It felt as impossible as Mateo's proposal, as her arrival in Kallyria, as her over-the-top wedding. Just another moment that she couldn't compute in this crazy life of hers.

'Get her in the car,' Matthias growled into his mouthpiece, and Rachel saw another guard emerge from behind an SUV with blacked-out windows, and Matthias started to hand her off.

Then she heard a sizzle and a crack and the next thing she knew the world had exploded.

Mateo could not ignore the tension banding his temples and tightening his gut as he tried to focus on the briefing one of his cabinet ministers was giving.

There was no reason to feel particularly anxious about Rachel's visit to the bazaar, but he did. Maybe it was a sixth sense. Maybe it was just paranoia. Or maybe it was the fact that he was finally acknowledging to himself that he cared about Rachel. Hell, he might even love her, and this was the result. This gut-twisting fear. This sense that he could never relax, never rest, never even breathe.

Love was fear. Love was failure. Love was dealing with both for ever, and it was why, after his experience with Cressida, he'd chosen never to pursue that dangerous, deadly emotion again.

Yet like the worst of enemies, it had come for him anyway.

'Your Highness…'

Mateo blinked the minister back into focus, realising he'd stopped speaking some moments ago, and everyone was waiting for him to respond.

'Thank you,' he said gruffly, shuffling some papers in front of him, hating how distracted he was. How he couldn't stop thinking of Rachel, for good or ill, for better or worse. Just like the marriage vows he'd made.

But it wasn't supposed to be this way.

He'd been so sure, when he'd first come up with his great plan, that with Rachel he'd be immune. He'd had ten years of inoculation, after all. How could he possibly fall in love with her after all that time together? How could he barely keep his hands off her, when for an entire decade he hadn't even considered touching her?

How had everything changed since their vows had been spoken, most of all himself? Because loving Rachel felt both as natural as breathing, as terrifying as deliberately stepping off a cliff.

He was already in free fall, because he knew it was too late. He already loved her. He'd been fighting it for weeks now, fighting it and revelling in it at the same time, to his own confusion and despair.

He knew Rachel saw the struggle in him, just

as he knew she was patiently waiting for him to resolve it. He saw the hope in her eyes when she looked at him, and that made everything worse, because he knew he was going to disappoint her, no matter what.

'Your Highness.'

He'd stopped listening to the conversation again. Irritated with himself beyond all measure, Mateo made himself focus on the minister again, only to realise he wasn't the one speaking.

A guard who had entered the stateroom was, and Mateo suddenly felt as if he'd been plunged underwater, as if everything were at a distance and he could only hear every third word. *Bazaar...bomb...wounded.*

He lurched up from the table, panic icing his insides, making it hard to breathe. Impossible to think. Rachel was in danger...and it was his fault. He'd been here before. He knew *exactly* how this felt.

'Is she alive?' he rasped.

'She's being taken to the hospital—'

'Get me there,' Mateo commanded, and he strode out of the room.

Half an hour later he was at the Royal Hospital on the outskirts of the city, the wintry fog obscuring the view of the terracotta roofs and onion domes of his city, his kingdom, so all was grey.

On the way there Rachel's security team had

briefed him on what had happened—a clumsy, homemade bomb thrown into the bazaar; the explosion had hurled Rachel in the air and she'd hit her head on a concrete kerb. Two other people had received non-life-threatening injuries, including her personal bodyguard, Matthias; they were both being treated.

'And the Queen?' Mateo demanded. 'How is she?'

'She sustained an injury to the head,' the doctor, an olive-skinned man with kind eyes, was telling him, although Mateo found it hard to listen to a word he said. His mind kept skittering back to other doctors, other sterile rooms, the awful surreal sensation of hearing what had happened and knowing he was to blame. Just him.

There was nothing we could do...so sorry... by the time she made it to the hospital, it was too late.

'Is she in a coma?' Mateo asked brusquely. 'Is there...brain damage?'

The doctor looked at him strangely and Mateo gritted his teeth. He couldn't bear not knowing. He couldn't bear being in the same place, knowing the life of the woman he loved was hanging in the balance, and it was all because of him. 'Well?' he demanded in a throaty rasp.

'She is conscious, Your Highness,' the doctor said, looking unnerved by his sovereign's unprecedented display of emotion. 'She regained consciousness almost immediately.' Mateo stared at him, not comprehending. Not possibly being able to understand what this meant. 'She needed to have six stitches to a cut on her forehead,' the doctor continued, 'but other than that she is fine.'

'Stitches?' Mateo repeated dumbly.

'She might have a small scar by her left eyebrow,' the doctor said in an apologetic tone, and Mateo just stared.

Stitches? Her *eyebrow*?

'She's…?' He found he could barely speak. 'She's not…?'

The doctor smiled then, seeming to understand the nature of Mateo's fear. 'She's fine. I will take you to her, if you like.'

Mateo found he could only nod.

A few minutes later he walked into a private room where Rachel was sitting up in bed, looking tired and a bit exasperated.

'I'm quite sure I don't need to stay overnight,' she was telling one of the nurses who fussed around her. *'Den... Chei... Efharisto...'*

He almost smiled at her halting attempts at Greek, which the nurses resolutely ignored with cheerful smiles, but he felt too emotional to manage it. He stood in the doorway and simply drank her in, his heart beating hard from the adrenalin rush of believing, of being so *certain*, she was in danger. Of thinking he was to blame.

Rachel turned and caught sight of him, smiling wryly. 'No one seems to be listening to me,' she said with a little shrug of her shoulders. Her gaze clouded as she caught the look on his face, although Mateo didn't even know what it was. 'Mateo…'

He didn't answer. He simply walked over to her and kissed her hard on the mouth. The nurses scattered like a flock of sparrows.

Mateo eased back and studied the six neat stitches by her eyebrow.

She was all right.

'I'll have quite a cool scar,' Rachel joked uncertainly, looking at him with worry in her eyes.

'I thought you were dead.'

Her lovely, lush mouth turned downward as she realised what he'd gone through, although of course she didn't realise at all. 'Oh, Mateo…'

He shook his head, the remembered emotion, the absolute terror of it, closing his throat. 'Dead,' he forced out, 'or in a coma. A traumatic brain injury…'

'Barely more than a graze.' Her fingers fluttered on his wrist. 'I'm okay, Mateo.'

Now that he knew she was all right, he couldn't escape the awful knowledge that this could have been so much worse…just as it could have been avoided. 'I knew it was dangerous.'

She shook her head. 'It wasn't the rebels. Just some poor deranged man acting on his own. No one could have predicted—'

'This time.'

'Mateo—'

'You should never have gone to the bazaar. I shouldn't have let you.' The words came out savagely, a rod for his own back.

'You can't keep me in a cage, you know.' Rachel's voice was deliberately light as her concerned gaze scanned his face. Mateo had no idea what she saw there. He felt as if he were a jumble of disparate parts; he'd been so terrified, and then so relieved, and now, inexplicably, he felt possessed by a fearsome, towering rage. He wanted to shout at the doctors. He wanted to tear apart the lone assailant with his bare hands. He wanted to hold Rachel and never let her go.

As the feelings coursed through him, each one more powerful and frightening than the last, he knew he couldn't handle this tempestuous seesaw of emotions any more. He couldn't live with the endless cycle of fear, relief, hope and guilt that had been his two years with Cressida. It had left him a husk of a man fifteen years ago, and he couldn't bear to have it happen again. He couldn't bear for Rachel to see it…or worse, far worse, for her not to see it, because one time it *wouldn't* be six stitches above her eyebrow.

This was what love wrought—grief and guilt, fear and failure. And he didn't want any part of it. He couldn't.

Rachel pressed her hand against Mateo's cheek and he closed his eyes. 'It's okay, Mateo.'

'It isn't.' He opened his eyes and stared at her, imprinting her on his brain, his heart. 'I can't do this,' he said, and he walked out of the room.

CHAPTER SIXTEEN

IT HAD BEEN raining for over a week. It was late November, and Kallyria was in the grip of the worst weather the island had seen in a century, or so her staff had told Rachel.

She liked the rain; it fitted her mood. It reminded her of England, and of everything she'd left behind. And while she couldn't bring herself to regret the choice she'd made, she still felt sad about it.

Ever since the day in the bazaar, Mateo had changed. When he'd walked out of her hospital proclaiming he couldn't do this—and Rachel was frankly terrified to ask him what 'this' meant—he'd kept his distance. The fledgling feeling that she'd been hoping had been growing between them seemed to have withered at the root, before it had had a chance to blossom.

And yet it had blossomed for her; she was in love with him, had been slowly and surely falling in love with him since their wedding, or, really, before then. Really, Rachel acknowledged to herself, she'd been falling in love with him since she'd first met him, when he'd introduced himself as her research partner and her breath had caught in her chest.

For ten years she'd kept herself from falling, because she knew, of *course* she knew, how impossible a relationship between them could be. Yet he'd asked her to marry him, and made her feel beautiful, and even though the kind of relationship she really wanted still felt impossible, she knew the truth.

She loved him. And he didn't love her back. Worse than that, far worse, was that he was choosing not to love her. Actively. Intentionally. And it was that knowledge, rather than him not loving her at all, that was bringing her closer to true despair than she'd ever felt before.

'So we have a round-table discussion today,' Francesca said, bustling into Rachel's bedroom with a briskly officious air and a quick smile. 'And a private engagement with the head of a girls' school tomorrow…'

'Right.' Rachel managed a tired smile. At least, she hoped she did. She hadn't slept well last night, with Mateo lying so silent and stony behind her, and she wondered if she ever would again. *'I can't do this,'* he'd said two weeks ago. Well, neither could she.

Francesca looked at her closely. 'Is everything all right? You're looking a bit peaky.'

Rachel just shrugged. As close a confidante as her stylist had become, she wasn't willing to share this particular heartache.

'Is it PMT?' Francesca asked sympathetically. 'I think it's that time of the month, isn't it?' Rachel stared at her blankly and she gave her an impish little smile. 'One of the things it helps to keep track of, when considering your wardrobe choices.'

Rachel's mind ticked over and she shook her head. 'I don't have PMT.'

'No?' Francesca was already in the enormous walk-in wardrobe that was now filled with clothes for a queen.

'I'm late,' Rachel said quietly. And she was never late. Of course, it shouldn't surprise her. She and Mateo had not been using any birth control, since he'd been upfront for his need for an heir as soon as possible. And yet somehow, in the midst of all the busyness of being, Rachel had forgotten she could fall pregnant. Mateo seemed to have forgotten it as well, for he'd certainly never mentioned it.

And yet here she was, just two months into her marriage, and her period six days late. She shouldn't be shocked, and yet she was.

'I was thinking something bright today,' Francesca said. 'To make you stand out in this endless rain…' She brandished a canary-yellow coat dress Rachel had never worn before. 'What do you think?'

Could she really be pregnant? And how would she find out? Rachel's mind raced. She couldn't exactly pop out to the nearest chemist's, at least not without a security detail and half the palace staff knowing what she was up to.

She glanced at Francesca. 'Francesca, can you be discreet?'

Her stylist didn't miss a beat as she answered, 'My middle name.'

'Could you go to the chemist for me?'

'The chemist?' Francesca's eyes narrowed. 'What for?'

Rachel swallowed dryly. 'A pregnancy test.'

Francesca, to her credit, merely gave a swift nod. 'Of course.'

Just twenty minutes later, Rachel knew. It felt strangely surreal to perch on the edge of the sunken marble tub in the adjoining bathroom and wait the requisite three minutes to read the test. She'd never taken one before, and she'd spent ten minutes studying the instructions before she'd done what she'd needed to do.

And now she had turned over the little stick, seen the two blazing pink lines, and knew. She was pregnant.

'This is good news, yes?' Francesca asked cautiously as Rachel came out of the bathroom. She knew the expression on her face wasn't one of undiluted joy. 'The King needs an heir…'

'Yes, it's good news.' Her voice sounded a bit wooden.

'You want to be a mother?' the stylist pressed.

'Yes.' Rachel was sure of that. She might have given up on the hope of motherhood years ago, when her romantic possibilities had been nil, but one of the reasons she'd said yes to Mateo's unconventional proposal had been for the possibility of children.

'So…' Francesca waited for Rachel to fill in the blanks, but she couldn't. She didn't want to talk of something so private and sacred to anyone—but Mateo. And she didn't know what she was going to say to him.

She spent all afternoon in a daze, going through the motions of her meetings, her mind elsewhere. Mateo was engaged on other business until the evening, so it wasn't until dinner that she had the chance to talk to him, and by that time she was resolved.

Agathe was otherwise engaged, which meant it was just her and Mateo in one of the palace's smaller dining rooms, the curtains drawn against the night and the rain, candles flickering on the table between them.

A member of staff served them the first course and withdrew. They were seated at opposite ends of the table that seated twelve, a dozen silver dishes between them along with all that hadn't been said.

Rachel gazed at her husband's face and felt an ache of longing for how she'd hoped for things to be. Oh, how she'd hoped. And yet one glance at Mateo's set jaw forced her to acknowledge that those were all they'd ever be. Hopes. Disappointed hopes.

They ate the first course in silence, as had become their habit in recent weeks, and Rachel tried to work up the courage to say what was on her mind—and heart.

Finally, when their main course had been delivered, she forced herself to speak.

'Mateo, I need to talk to you.'

He looked up, his expression already guarded. 'Yes?'

'Two weeks ago you left my room at the hospital, saying, "I can't do this."' She paused, waiting for him to respond, or say anything, but he simply remained silent, his jaw tense, his eyes narrowed. 'What was it you couldn't do, Mateo?'

'Why are you asking?'

'Don't I have a right to know?'

He sighed, the sound impatient. 'Rachel…'

'You've been shutting me out ever since then,' Rachel stated with quiet, trembling dignity. 'Did you expect me not to notice? Not to *care*?' Her voice caught on a wavering note and she sucked in a quick breath, determined to stay composed.

Mateo laid his hands flat on the table. 'No, of course not. I'm sorry. I know… I know I'm not being fair to you.'

'But you'll do it anyway?'

'The truth is, I don't know how to be.' The look of naked vulnerability on his face seared her heart. 'I don't… I don't know how to love someone. And if that's what you want…'

'Don't know? Or don't want to?'

He hesitated, a familiar, obdurate cast on his features. 'Both, I suppose.'

'Why?'

'I don't want to hurt you—'

'You already have,' Rachel cut across him, trying to sound matter-of-fact and not bitter. 'So if that's your only reason…'

'Why can't we be happy the way we were?' Mateo said. 'As friends.'

'Because you're not acting like my friend, Mateo. You're acting cold and stony and basically a big, fat jerk.' He let out a huff of surprised laughter and Rachel squared her shoulders, knowing what more she needed to say, even if saying it would break her heart clean in half.

'I've been thinking about this quite a lot lately,' she said quietly. 'About you and me, and whether I'd be happy to live without love.'

'I do care for you—'

'But the thing is,' Rachel interjected sadly, 'you don't want to. You're fighting it. Fighting me. Maybe it's because you loved someone before and it hurt. I understand that, Mateo. You've lost a lot of people in your life. Your father, your brother.' She paused. 'Cressida.' Mateo did not reply, but his eyes flashed and his jaw tightened. Even now he couldn't bear to have her name mentioned, and that felt like the saddest thing of all.

'What I'm saying is, I'm not going to fight you back. Part of me wants to, a large part. To fight for you, for *us*. But the funny thing is…' her voice wavered and almost caught on a sob that she managed to hold back '… I'm not going to, because you made me feel I was worth more than that. All my life I've tried to make myself useful or needed, because I'd convinced myself that was almost as good as being loved. I told you my parents didn't love me, and I made myself not mind, because it was easier that way. They weren't bad people, really. They loved their jobs and their social life and they didn't really want an awkward, nerdy girl messing it all up.'

Mateo opened his mouth and Rachel held up a hand to keep him from interrupting. 'I'm not saying this to gain your pity. I really don't want that. I'm just trying to explain. Between them and the whole thing with Josh…well, you were the first person in my life who made me feel I was worth loving.'

'Rachel…'

'You made me feel beautiful and lovely and lovable. And you woke me up to the reality that I shouldn't have to settle for anything less.'

Mateo's eyes widened as he stared at her. 'What are you saying?'

'Don't worry,' she said calmly. She felt empty inside, now that it was all being said. 'I'm not going to leave you. I made vows, and I know my duty. I will stay by your side, as your Queen.' Another breath, to buoy her. This felt like the hardest part. 'But I'm not going to try any longer, Mateo. I'm not going to try to make you love me, and I'm going to do my best not to love you back. It's too hard to handle the ups and downs—the days when you decide to relax enough to let me in, and then the days when you don't.'

'I don't…' Mateo began helplessly, shaking his head. He looked shell-shocked.

'It's not fair on me,' Rachel stated, 'and it wouldn't be fair on our child. Because that is something else I've realised. I don't want a child of mine growing up thinking one of their parents doesn't love them.'

'I would love my child,' Mateo declared in a near growl.

'Would you? How can I possibly believe or trust that?'

'Because—'

'You don't have a great track record,' Rachel cut across him. 'But I accept that you will be involved in our child's life.'

'Of *course* I will—'

'But as for us, I want us to live separately. I'll still live in the palace, but in a separate wing. I'll continue with my own interests and charitable causes, and I'll appear with you in public, but privately we won't spend time together or have a relationship.'

'What…?' Mateo's mouth gaped open as he stared at her. 'But…'

'I think you'll find this works best for both of us,' Rachel said firmly, even though she felt as if her heart were being torn into little pieces and then stamped on. How could this be better? And yet how could she survive otherwise?

'We're married, Rachel—'

'A marriage of convenience only.'

'I still need an heir—'

'That's no longer an issue,' Rachel told him woodenly. 'Because I'm pregnant.'

Mateo stared at Rachel, his mind spinning uselessly, as she told him she was expecting his child and then rose from the table and walked out of the dining room with stiff, wounded dignity.

He slumped back in his chair, hardly able to take it all in. Rachel living separately from him. Trying not to love him.

Pregnant with his child...

A sound close to a moan escaped him as he raked his hands through his hair. How had this happened? And why did he not feel relieved—that Rachel was suggesting exactly the sort of arrangement that should suit him? No complications. No messy emotions. No danger, no risk, no guilt or grief.

This should be exactly what he wanted, but in that moment Mateo knew it wasn't. It wasn't what he wanted at *all*. Instead of feeling relieved, he was gutted. Eviscerated, as if the heart of him had been drawn right out, replaced by an empty shell, the wind whistling through him.

He didn't know how long he sat there, his mind and heart both empty, but eventually a member of staff came to clear the plates, and Mateo stumbled out of the room.

He must have fallen asleep at some point in the night, although time seemed to have lost all meaning. He spent most of those endless hours simply staring into space, his mind empty of coherent thought and yet full of memories.

Memories of Rachel...ones he hadn't even realised he'd had, and yet now held so dear. The way she'd stick a pencil in her messy bun as she was working, and then forget she had it there and search for one uselessly around her until Mateo drew the stub out of her hair and handed it to her with a laugh.

Evenings at their local pub, him with a pint and her with a shandy—such a funny, old-fashioned drink—testing each other on the periodic table. She'd come up with the game first, insisting she could name all the elements faster than he could. Even though he'd won that first time, they'd continued to play the game, finding it funnier with each playing.

And then later, far sweeter memories—Rachel in her wedding gown, her heart in her eyes, and then Rachel with nothing on at all, her hair spread out in a dark wave against the pillow as she looked up at him with so much trust and desire and love.

Yes, love. She loved him. He knew that; he felt it, just as he felt his own love for her, like a river or a force field, something that couldn't be controlled. Why didn't he just stop fighting it?

'Mateo.' His mother's gentle voice broke into his thoughts, and Mateo looked up, surprised to see his mother in the doorway of his study. Had he gone to bed? He couldn't even remember, but sunlight was now streaming through the windows, the fog finally breaking apart.

'What time is it?' he asked as he scrubbed his eyes and tried to clear the cobwebs from his mind.

'Seven in the morning. Have you slept at all?'

'I don't know.'

Agathe came into the room, her smile sorrowful and sympathetic as her gaze swept over her son. 'Is it Rachel?' she asked quietly.

'How did you know?'

'I have been watching you both all this time, and seeing how you love one another. Knowing you would fight it.'

'I made such a mess of my last relationship,' Mateo said in a low voice. 'My love was toxic.' He choked the words, barely able to get them out.

'Mateo, that wasn't your fault.'

'Wasn't it?' He stared at her hopelessly. '*She* said it was.'

'Cressida was a fragile, damaged individual,' Agathe said gently. 'Her death was not your fault. And,' she continued firmly, 'Rachel is not Cressida. She's strong, and she knows her own mind.'

'She's leaving me.'

'What…?'

'Not properly,' he amended as he scrubbed his

eyes. 'We'll remain married. But she wants us to live separate lives.'

'Ah.' Agathe nodded slowly. 'I was afraid of something like this.'

'Were you?' Mateo dropped his fists from his eyes to look at his mother, the weariness and memory etched into every line of her face.

'It's not easy to love someone who doesn't love you back quite as much, or even at all.'

It took Mateo a moment to make sense of his mother's meaning. 'Do you mean Father…?'

'The Karavitis men are strong and stubborn. They don't want to need anybody.'

'But you had such a successful marriage.'

'There are different definitions of success. I choose to believe in one that is about love and happiness, as well as duty and service.'

'I'm sorry,' Mateo said after a moment. 'I never knew.'

'We were happy, in our way,' Agathe said. 'I learned to be happy. But I want more for you… and for Rachel.'

'So do I,' Mateo said, his voice throbbing with the strength of his feeling. 'That's why…'

'Oh, Mateo. Do you honestly think she'd be happy without you?'

'She doesn't know—'

'Then tell her,' Agathe urged, her voice full of sorrow and love. 'For heaven's sake, tell her.'

* * *

He found her in the gardens. The fog had finally lifted, and the day was crisp and clear, the sun surprisingly warm as it shone down on the rain-washed gardens.

Mateo had gone to her suite of rooms first, and everything in him had lurched at the sight of several blank-faced members of staff moving her things out.

'Where are you putting those?' he'd demanded hoarsely, and someone had told him Queen Rachel was intending to reside in the south wing, about as far from him as possible. He felt both angry and lost, and yet he couldn't blame her.

So he'd left her rooms and gone to the south wing, but she wasn't there either, and when Francesca had told him, a look of naked pity on her face, that Rachel had wanted some fresh air, he'd come out here, and now he'd found her, in a small octagonal-shaped rose garden, the branches now pruned back and bare.

'Rachel.' His voice sounded hoarse and he cleared his throat. 'Rachel,' he said again, and she looked up.

'Mateo.'

'You're having your things moved.' It wasn't what he wanted to say, but he couldn't manage anything else right then.

'I told you I would.'

'I know.' He took a step towards her. She was sitting on a stone bench by a fountain that had filled with autumn leaves. Her hair was back in a plait and she was wearing a forest-green turtleneck in soft, snug cashmere and a grey skirt. She looked every inch the Queen, every bit his wife, and so wonderfully beautiful. *His.* She had to be his.

'I don't want you to,' he said and she started to shake her head. 'Please. Hear me out. I heard everything you said last night, and I've been thinking about nothing else since. But now...now I want a turn to tell you about what I've been thinking.'

A guarded expression came over her face, and she nodded. 'All right.'

Mateo moved to sit down next to her on the bench. 'You told me how your parents shaped how you felt about yourself. Well, in a fashion, mine did as well. I knew I was loved—I never doubted that. But I didn't feel important.'

'Because you weren't the heir?'

'My parents thought they were doing me a kindness, and I suppose in a way they were. They shielded me from all the intensity and pressure of the royal life. They gave me the freedom to pursue my own dreams—which led me to chemistry, and Cambridge, and you.' He swallowed hard. 'But I suppose I struggled with feeling a bit less than. I rebelled as a child, and then I turned away from all things royal. And then I met Cressida.'

Rachel's eyes widened as she gazed at him. 'You're going to tell me about her?'

'Yes, I'm going to tell you about her.' He took a deep breath, willing himself to begin, to open the old wounds and let them bleed out. 'Cressida was…fragile. She'd had a difficult if privileged upbringing and she liked—she needed—people to take care of her. I liked that at first. When I was with her, I felt important. I was eighteen, young and foolish, and Cressida made me feel like I was essential to her well-being. I craved that feeling of someone needing me absolutely. It stroked my ego, I'm ashamed to say.'

'That's understandable,' Rachel murmured. Her gaze was still guarded.

'But then she became unstable.' He shook his head, impatient with himself. 'Or, more to the point, I realised she was unstable. I should have seen it earlier. The warning signs were all there, but I thought that was just Cressida. How she was.'

'What happened?' Rachel asked softly.

'Her moods swung wildly. Something I said, something seemingly insignificant, could send her into a depression for days. She wouldn't even tell me what it was—I had to guess, and I usually got it wrong.' He paused, the memories of so desperately trying to make Cressida feel better, and never being able to, reverberating through him. 'I tried so hard, but it was never enough. She spiralled into severe depression on several occasions. I'll spare you some of the more harrowing details, but she started hurting herself, or going days without speaking or even getting up from bed. Her grades started to suffer—she was studying English—and she was close to being sent down from university.'

'That sounds so difficult,' Rachel murmured. Mateo couldn't tell from her tone whether she truly empathised with him or not. She looked cautious, as if she didn't know what was coming.

'It was incredibly complicated. I wanted to break up with her, but I was afraid to—both for her sake and mine. We'd become so caught up in one another, so dependent. It wasn't healthy, and it didn't make either of us happy, and I don't think it was really love at all.' Even though it had felt like it at the time, and made him never want to experience it again. 'But it consumed us, in its way, and then…' A pause while he gathered his courage. 'In our third year, Cressida killed herself.'

Rachel let out a soft gasp. 'Oh, Mateo…'

'She left a note,' he continued in a hard voice he didn't recognise as his own. Hard and bleak. 'I found it. I found *her*. She'd overdosed on antidepressants and alcohol—I rushed her to the hospital, but it was too late. That's why, I think, I acted so crazily when you were at the hospital. I was right back there, fearing Cressida was dead, and then knowing she was.'

'I'm so sorry…'

'But you know what the note said? It said she was killing herself because of me. Because I made her so unhappy.' His throat had thickened but he forced himself to go on. 'And you know what? She was right. I did make her unhappy. I must have done, because when she was gone, for a second I felt relieved.' His voice choked as he gasped out the words, 'How could I have felt that? What kind of man feels that?' He'd never told anyone that before. Never dared to reveal the shameful secret at the very heart of himself, but Rachel didn't recoil or even blink.

'Oh, Mateo.' Her face softened in sympathy as her arms came around him and he rested his face against her shoulder, the hot press of tears against his lids.

'I'm so sorry,' she whispered, one hand resting on his hair. 'So, so sorry.'

'I'm the one who's sorry,' Mateo said raggedly, swallowing down the threat of tears. He eased back, determined to look at her as he said these words. 'You're right, Rachel, I have been fighting you. I'm scared to love you, scared *for* you. I don't want to make you unhappy, and I don't want to feel the guilt and grief of knowing that I did.'

'Love is a two-way street, Mateo,' Rachel said gently. 'You don't bear the sole responsibility for my happiness. What you had with Cressida…'

'I know it wasn't really love. It was toxic and childish and incredibly dysfunctional. I know that. I've known that for a long time. But you can know one thing and feel something else entirely.'

'Yes,' Rachel agreed quietly. 'You can.'

'But when you left me last night—left me emotionally if not physically—I felt as if you'd died. I felt even more bereft than when I lost Cressida, and without that treacherous little flicker of relief. I was just…grief-stricken.'

Rachel stared at him, searching his face. 'What…what are you saying?' she finally asked.

'That I love you. That I've been falling in love with you for ten years without realising it, and then fighting it for the last few weeks when I started to understand how hard I'd fallen. But I don't want to fight any more. I know I'll get things wrong, and I'm terrified of hurting you, but I want to love you, Rachel. I want to live a life of loving you. If…if…you do love me.'

Rachel let out a sound, half laugh, half sob. 'Of course I love you. I think I fell in love with you a long time ago, but I tried to stop myself. Maybe we're not so different in that respect.' She gave a trembling laugh as she wiped the tears from her eyes.

'Maybe we're not.' Mateo took her hands in his. 'Can you forgive me, Rachel? For fighting you for so long, and hurting you in the process? I was trying not to hurt you, but I knew I was. I'm a fool.'

'As long as you're a love-struck fool, I don't mind,' she promised him as she squeezed his hands.

'I am,' Mateo assured her solemnly. 'Utterly and overwhelmingly in love with you. Now and for always. I know it doesn't mean everything will be perfect, or that we'll never hurt each other, but I really do love you.'

'And I love you,' Rachel told him. 'More than I ever thought possible. Getting to know you these last weeks…it's made me realise how much I love you. And if you love me back…'

'I do.'

'Then that's all that matters. That's what will get us through the ups and downs. That's what will last.'

'Yes, it will,' Mateo agreed, and then leaned forward to kiss her. He settled his mouth softly on hers, and it felt as if he was finally coming home, the two of them together, now and for ever.

EPILOGUE

Three years later

'MAMA, MAMA, LOOK at me!'

Rachel laughed and clapped her hands as her daughter, Daphne, ran towards her, her dark hair tumbling over her shoulders, her blue-green eyes alight with happiness and mischief.

It was a bright, sunny day, the sky picture-postcard-blue, the white sand of Kallyria's famous beaches stretching out before them. They were holidaying at the royal summer palace on the western coast of Kallyria. In the three years since Mateo had taken the crown, he'd dealt with the insurgents, stabilised the country's economy, and been a leader in bringing Kallyria into a modern and progressive world. It hadn't always been easy, but Rachel had been with him every step of the way.

She'd expanded into the role of Queen with energy and grace, not in small part down to Mateo's unwavering support and love. She'd also taken a six-week research position at the university in Athens last year, which he'd wholeheartedly supported.

But her heart was in Kallyria with her King and her family, and she knew there was nowhere else she'd rather be.

A year ago her mother had died, and Rachel had had the privilege of being with her at the end. To her surprise, although her mother hadn't remembered who she was in months, she'd turned to her suddenly, grasping her hand with surprising vigour, and said, 'I'm sorry. Do you know that, Rachel? That I'm sorry?'

And Rachel, with tears in her eyes, had said she had.

Now she scooped up her daughter and pressed her lips to her sun-warmed cheek, revelling in the simple joy of the moment. From behind her she heard Mateo coming through the French windows of the palace that led directly onto the beach.

'This one's up and ready for his mama.'

With a smile Rachel exchanged armfuls with her husband—he took Daphne and she took her three-month-old son, Kosmos, who nuzzled into her neck.

'Come on, *moraki mou*,' he said cheerfully as he tossed Daphne over his shoulder and tickled her tummy. 'Time for lunch.'

'And this one is ready for lunch too,' Rachel said as she followed him inside.

Sunlight streamed across the floor and Mateo caught her eye as he settled Daphne at the table, and Rachel curled up on the sofa to feed Kosmos.

The look he gave her was lingering, full of love as well as promise. Was it possible to be this happy? This thankful? This amazed?

Meeting her husband's loving gaze, feeling the warmth of it right down to her toes, Rachel knew it was, and with her heart full to bursting she smiled back.

* * * * *